THE BATTLE
FOR THE CASTLE

Elizabeth Winthrop

the author of *The Castle in the Attic*

A Yearling Book

For all my Williams, both real and imaginary

Published by
Dell Yearling
an imprint of
Random House Children's Books
a division of
Random House, Inc.
1540 Broadway
New York, New York 10036

Visit us on the Web! www.randomhouse.com

Educators and librarians, for a variety of teaching tools, visit us at www.randomhouse.com/teachers

Check out Elizabeth Winthrop's Web site!
www.absolutesway.com/winthrop

ISBN: 0-440-40942-X

Reprinted by arrangement with Holiday House, Inc.

Printed in the United States of America

December 1994

OPM   20   19

If we do not redefine manhood, war is inevitable.

—*Paul Fussell*

ACKNOWLEDGMENTS

Each book has its own special circle of friends and supporters. For this one I would like to thank Keith McDaniels and Jan Perkins, who listened patiently while I struggled with the underpinnings of this story. Thanks to Frank DeCrescenzo, who told me how he "jumped the trains." And to Henry Chapin, for his insightful meditations on the ways and the history of fools. Tom Hart's knowledge of bicycles was invaluable.

Margery Cuyler is an enthusiastic and persevering editor. Without her unflagging encouragement, this book truly would not have been written. And last but never least, thanks to Alison Cragin Herzig, who helps me find my way back to the path whenever I wander astray.

—ELIZABETH WINTHROP
September 1992

THE BATTLE
FOR THE CASTLE

CHAPTER 1

"They sure move fast, don't they?" William said as the freight train barreled down the track toward them.

Jason nodded. "It looks that way from here. But they slow up as they come into the station." The whistle blew and the engineer waved at the two boys as he swept past. "See, he's braking now," Jason yelled over the roar of the passing cars. "That's the trick. You start running alongside as soon as the engineer puts on the brakes. That way you're in the rhythm of it when you grab the ladder and swing yourself up. It's all in the timing."

Timing, William thought. At least he knew about that from gymnastics. Timing, balance, flexibility. He had all those. But he was still a shrimp. He and Jason used to be the same size but in the last year, his best friend had grown a foot. What if I can't even reach the ladder? William thought. Or worse, what if I'm not strong enough to pull myself up? I'll just be dragged along like a sack of potatoes until I fall off.

"See, here come the boxcars," Jason called. "They have a ladder at each end. I'll grab the first and you get the second."

William tried to look happy about all this, but deep down he had a weird feeling in his stomach. They'd been waiting their whole lives to jump the trains. They'd always sworn they'd do it together. Next Saturday was the day because it fell on the first weekend after William's twelfth birthday.

Jumping the trains. It meant you ran along next to the train, grabbed the ladder on the side of a boxcar, scrambled over the top of the car, and threw yourself off the other side before the train picked up speed at the far end of Southbrook station. Jumping the trains was a rite of passage for all the boys in town. You did it when you turned twelve. Nobody knew who started it and nobody could figure out how to stop it. The school principal gave speeches about how dangerous it was, and for a while, the police and the parents set up patrols along the tracks to keep the kids from doing it. But nothing worked. If you hadn't jumped the trains by the time you were thirteen, you were nobody.

William glanced at his friend. Ever since Jason got

that new mountain bike for his birthday in March, he'd changed. Jason the piano player and the champion parakeet trainer and the first guy in their class to get glasses and William's best friend had suddenly turned into a bike freak and a muscleman. He trained every day. He had all the right equipment—the special black helmet, the riding gloves, a little tool kit that fit under the seat. After school he put on some really weird-looking black shiny shorts and pedaled off on some long course he'd worked out with his father. Jason's father was an exercise nut. Some days they went twenty miles, and more on the weekends. Then they came home and did a hundred sit-ups or something. Whenever Jason had a chance, he showed William his muscles.

"So, it's a deal," Jason said. "We meet here next Saturday morning." He stuck out his hand and William shook it solemnly. Then Jason gave a little whoop and punched him on the shoulder. "We're finally going to jump the trains. And man, we're ready for it. I've got all my biking muscles and you're in great shape. After all, you've been doing gymnastics since you were six years old."

"Yeah, and I'm about to quit."

They headed back toward their bikes. "You've been talking about quitting for ages," Jason said.

"This time I mean it," William said. "I don't like

this new woman who's coaching the team. Most of the other guys have already given up.''

''What would you do instead?''

''I don't know,'' William said. That was the problem. He hated baseball. He was much too short for basketball. Track seemed really boring. At least in gymnastics he was still a star.

''You'd be dumb to quit,'' Jason said as he lifted his bike and twirled the wheels a couple of times. ''You're the best one at floor routines. Everybody says so.''

''Yeah, but they think gymnastics is wimpy.''

Jason grinned. ''Wimpy? Why don't they try it?'' William had once tried to teach Jason a simple front walkover in the living room. After six tries, Jason had finally flipped his legs to the other side, but in the process, he'd knocked over his mother's favorite lamp. ''Definitely not my sport,'' was all he'd said as they swept the broken china into the dustpan. In those days, Jason didn't have a sport. But he sure does now, William thought as he watched his friend checking the gears on his twenty-one-speed bike.

They started off together, but as usual Jason pulled ahead on the long hill above the train station. He waited at the top for William to catch up.

''That old bike of yours is a joke,'' Jason said. ''I hope your parents get you a new one for your birthday.''

William took a minute to catch his breath before

answering. "Me too. Dad just signed the contract to design a new housing development so they're feeling okay about money."

"Did you take him to the bike store and show him the one we picked out?" Jason asked.

"We went yesterday after school," William said. "He didn't understand why I needed such a fancy bike."

"It'll last a long time. And it's got the thicker tires if we want to go off-road, but it's light enough to take the hills easily. You know, Dad signed me up for a two-week biking trip in Nova Scotia in July," Jason added. "If you get your bike and start a regular training program, you'd be in shape to go too. That would be great."

"You never told me you were doing that," William said.

Jason shrugged. "Dad came up with the idea last week. He went on some camping trip to Nova Scotia when he was a kid, so now he wants me to do it."

"How's the great Ping-Pong war?" William asked.

"Dad's ahead by two games but I'm catching up." For six months, Jason and his father had been playing Ping-Pong in their basement every night. They kept track of all the games on a blackboard on the wall.

"You headed home?" William asked when they pulled up to the four-way light at Trafalgar.

"No. I think I'll do the course around the reservoir

now,'' Jason said. ''That'll get me up to thirty miles for today.''

''Don't forget my birthday dinner Friday night. I've got gymnastics practice that day so I'm busy till five.''

''Right,'' Jason said. ''Maybe I'll come watch your practice.''

''What?'' William asked. ''And give up some training time?''

''I like that new coach. She's pretty even though she's got fat legs.''

Jason had begun to talk about girls and the way they looked. It made William feel weird.

''Gymnasts need strong legs,'' he said as Jason pulled away.

Jason waved good-bye, then hunkered his body down into racing position and began to pump his way up Trafalgar to the reservoir.

When William came in the kitchen door, his mother was on the phone. ''Yes, Mrs. Roberts,'' she was saying. ''I know it's his third ear infection this year. Sometimes these things just settle in. Keep him on the antibiotics and bring him in first thing Monday.'' Pause. ''No, that's really not necessary . . .''

He poured himself a bowl of cereal. His mother waved at him, made an apologetic face at the phone, and then pointed to something on the kitchen table.

"It's your birthday present from Mrs. Phillips," she whispered with her hand over the receiver. Then she went back to little Harry Roberts's ear infections.

Mrs. Phillips had taken care of William from the day he was born until she moved back to England to live with her brother two years ago. She always sent good presents. This one was small, the size of a pack of cards, and it was wrapped in shiny brown-striped paper. She had printed his full name, William Edward Lawrence, in big block letters that filled up the label. One corner was covered in purple stamps with pictures of the queen on them. In the other corner, down near the bottom, it said, PERSONAL AND CONFIDENTIAL. DO NOT OPEN BEFORE MAY 5TH.

He picked up the package and shook it. Not a sound. Mrs. Phillips was a careful wrapper. He put it down again and studied it while he ate his cereal.

His mother hung up the phone. "Bet you wish you had X-ray vision," she said. "What do you think it is?"

"It's pretty small."

"A wallet?"

"Maybe," William said, but he didn't think so. Mrs. Phillips wouldn't send him something as boring as that. Not for his twelfth birthday. He tipped his bowl up and slurped down the last of the milk. His mother glared at him but she made no comment.

"I'm meeting your father in town," she said. "We'll be back in a couple of hours."

"Wouldn't you like me to come along?" teased William. He was pretty sure they were going to buy his birthday present.

"No, thanks," she said. "Not this time. Remember, no more handstands against the living room wall or else."

"I know, I know. Or else I'll have to clean off the footprints myself. Listen, Mom, you should be glad I don't do handstands in sneakers. Or that I didn't try to teach Jason front walkovers in *our* living room."

"I'm always grateful for small favors," his mother said as she went out the door.

When Mrs. Phillips had moved back to England two years ago, William had really missed her. He hated walking into the empty house after school. He'd turn on the radio as soon as he got home just so there'd be some noise to keep him company. But gradually he had gotten used to it. He could eat three bowls of cereal with nobody bugging him about snacks between meals. He could play his music as loud as he wanted to. He could even sneak some afternoon television.

He picked up the birthday package and turned it over in his fingers. Such a small box. It made him wonder. Did it have anything to do with the castle up in the attic, the one Mrs. Phillips had given him as a good-bye present? In the weeks after she left, he'd played with it all the time, but after a while he stopped going up there. Poor old castle, he thought with a sudden pang of guilt. Better go see it.

He left the present sitting in the middle of the table and headed up to the attic. In the fading afternoon light, he walked around the stone and wooden castle. It looked smaller to him than before. When Mrs. Phillips first showed it to him, he remembered thinking it was enormous. He knelt down to raise the drawbridge and drop the portcullis. Despite the thick layer of dust on all the surfaces, everything still worked. That was good. And the legend above the castle doors still read:

When the lady doth ply her needle
And the lord his sword doth test,
Then the squire shall cross the drawbridge
And the time will be right for a quest.

It had all come true. Or had it? Mrs. Phillips was the only other one who knew what happened. William hadn't even told Jason about his adventures in the castle. About Sir Simon, the little lead knight that had come to life and his magic token that shrunk people and Alastor, the evil wizard who tried to trap them all. William looked over his shoulder half expecting to see the path leading out of the attic into the forest, but of course there was nothing behind him but the shadowy shapes of old trunks and discarded furniture.

As he dusted off the outer walls of the castle with a rag from the corner bin, he tried to imagine what could be in Mrs. Phillips's neatly wrapped package. Another knight? Or maybe some furniture for the castle or a new roasting spit for the kitchen. Or the lead figure of Alastor. No, of course not. She had promised to throw both him and the token into the ocean.

It was getting dark. He stood up. Maybe the present had nothing to do with what had happened before. Or what might have happened. After all, Mrs. Phillips would know that he had outgrown the castle by now.

CHAPTER 2

On Friday afternoon, William was just getting on his bike when Jason swooped up behind him.

"Sorry I'm late. How was gymnastics practice?" Jason asked as they pushed off in unison.

"It was good you missed it. I got bawled out by the coach at the end for not concentrating."

He and Jason rode along in silence. Jason seemed to be trying out new riding positions or something. First he stuck his head out, then ducked it down and watched his feet turning on the pedals under him.

"What are you doing?" William asked at last.

"Stretching out my neck muscles. They cramp up if you hold one position too long."

"How was your time today?"

"Okay," Jason said. "Not as good as Dad wants."

"He really pushes you."

"Yeah, he does," Jason said. "But I need it. He's like my coach."

William was jealous. His father cooked Chinese food and listened to the opera and built strange things in the workshop that he usually forgot to finish. Maybe if he played baseball with William in the backyard or took him to football games at the university stadium, William would be tougher, more like the other guys. Maybe then he wouldn't be scared of jumping the trains.

William saved the biggest present for last. His father and mother had carried it in and leaned it against the wall of the dining room before dinner. There it sat under a sheet with a bright red ribbon tied around it. Jason could barely contain himself.

"Don't you want to open that one?" he asked twice during the meal.

"That's last," said William.

"No," Jason said as he picked up his own present from under a pile of ripped wrapping paper. "I want mine to be last."

"Then this is next," said William as he started in on the small tidily wrapped box from Mrs. Phillips. He ripped the paper off and tossed it on the floor. An envelope was taped to the top of the white cardboard box. In a thick black scrawl, Mrs. Phillips had written "Squire William" on it.

"What does she mean by that?" his mother asked, leaning over to see.

William didn't answer. He pushed his chair back from the table so he could read the letter to himself.

Dear William:

When Sir Simon and I put you through your training in the castle, he remarked to me that a ten-year-old was too young to be a squire. Twelve is the correct age. But of course, at that time, we had no choice if any of us were ever to get out of our predicament.

I send you this present because I trust you remember some of what I tried to teach you about love and courage and loyalty. This seems the proper weapon for a proper squire. Use it wisely and in good health.

With love,

Mrs. Phillips

P.S. I did throw Alastor into the ocean as I promised.

"You're driving us crazy," his father said. "What is it?"

William lifted the lid off the cardboard box. The

token, a medallion the size of a collar button, lay in a bed of cotton. Everybody crowded around.

"What is it?" his mother asked. She reached over to pick it up, but William slipped the cover back on the box before she had a chance.

"It's a very special button," he said. Jason shot him a look, but William just shook his head slightly as if to say, I'll explain later. Why had she sent it to him? he thought wildly. She was supposed to throw it into the ocean along with Alastor.

"William?" his mother said. Everybody was staring at him.

He shoved Mrs. Phillips's box deep into the pocket of his jeans and walked over to the big present leaning against the wall.

It wasn't the right bike. William knew it the moment he saw the size of the tires. And without turning around to look at his friend's face, he knew that Jason knew it too. William took his time rolling up the sheet and pretending to inspect the gears and the pedals.

"Gee, Mom and Dad, thanks so much. It's great," he said. "It's really great."

"We didn't get the one you two picked out, Jason," William's father explained. "Frankly, it was pretty expensive and the bike-store owner convinced us that this one would suit William's needs just fine. You're the expert. What do you think of it?"

Jason got up and walked over to the bike. He picked

it up, flipped it over, twirled the wheels. "Nice touring bike, Mr. Lawrence. Twelve speeds, lightweight. William's really going to go far on this little machine. . . . As long as he has smooth roads."

And all the time, William knew what he was really saying. This bike can't go off-road, these flimsy tires can't handle the reservoir path. No stamina, no endurance. No Nova Scotia.

William's mother began gathering up the wrapping paper. "How about your present, Jason?" she asked. "That's the last one to open before I bring in the cake."

"Oh, it's nothing, Dr. Lawrence. I'll show it to William later."

"Don't be silly. Why don't you open it, William, while your father and I are in the kitchen?"

As William unwrapped the two waterproof panniers, Jason said, "You'll have to take them back. They're too heavy for a racing bike. I got them for you so we could go on overnights together. You know, to get ready for the Nova Scotia trip."

William didn't know what to say.

"This bike is all wrong," Jason said. "The skinny wheels wouldn't last two seconds off-road. They may even slide out when you hit the gravel in your driveway. Here, give the panniers back. I'll get you the lighter-weight ones."

Suddenly the lights went out and everybody started

singing "Happy Birthday." As soon as he finished his cake, Jason said he had to go home.

William walked him out to his bike. Jason folded the panniers and shoved them inside his own.

"You heard what my father said," William said. "I guess they couldn't afford a fancy mountain bike like yours. Nova Scotia probably wouldn't have worked out anyway."

"Don't worry about it, okay?" Jason hopped on his bike and pushed off. "It's no big deal. See you."

"We're still jumping the trains tomorrow, right?" William called out after him.

"Sure," Jason said as he turned at the end of the driveway. "Meet me down there at eight."

"Hey, Jason," William shouted once more. But Jason didn't answer. He'd already gone around the corner.

William stood in the deepening darkness. He shoved his hands into the pockets of his jeans and closed his fingers around the small cardboard box. "Maybe I didn't want to go to stupid old Nova Scotia anyway," he said out loud to the air.

CHAPTER 3

The next morning William woke with a start. Through the slits in his venetian blinds, he could see that the sun wasn't even up yet. What was wrong?

The trains. Of course. This was the morning they were going to jump the trains. He wished he could blink and the day would be over. Then he'd already be done with the stupid trains and Jason wouldn't care that he didn't get the right bike for his birthday.

Mrs. Phillips told him it was good he was small. "All great gymnasts are small," she reminded him. "And being different is not such a bad thing. It gives you a gentle heart."

A lot of good that does me today, William thought. "A shrimpy kid with a gentle heart is not exactly your master train jumper, Mrs. P.," he said. He opened the drawer of his bedside table and reached toward the back for the cardboard box.

"This sure is one special button," he whispered as he took it out and turned it over. The two-sided token had the power to shrink living things and then bring them back to normal size. Both surfaces were decorated with the head of Janus, the god who looks both ways in time. He frowned on the shrinking side and smiled on the side that reversed the spell.

William checked his clock. Another hour till he had to meet Jason. He rummaged around for his magnifying glass and his flashlight. "Let's find out if you still work," he said, placing the token back in its box and kicking off his sheets.

The light bulb hanging from the attic ceiling was dim and covered with dust. William was glad he had remembered his flashlight. The animal he was looking for would be hiding in the deepest, darkest corners of the attic.

A mouse would be the best thing. Sir Simon used to zap them and roast them for dinner. William shuddered at the thought. But a mouse wouldn't be easy to find on such short notice, so he'd settled on a spider. Under the slanting eaves, behind two trunks, he discovered a large intricate web in the bottom half of one of the windows. The spider was resting, her slender legs splayed delicately across the strands of her net. William blew gently on the web to make sure she was alive. She skittered across to the other side. As he pulled the token and his magnifying glass out of his pajama pocket, she let herself down from the window-sill on a silk strand.

"Janus," he said, pointing the frowning face at her. In midair, she seemed to disappear completely, but he found her quickly enough with the magnifying glass. She was making her way across one of the wide floor-boards.

"It works," he cried. "It still works!" Then he sat back on his heels and stared out the window. So it all must have happened. Sir Simon and the castle and the road out of the attic.

Where had the spider gone? He had to find her and change her back to normal size. Even a spider shouldn't be left as small as that. He ran his magnify-ing glass back and forth along the floorboard. At last he found her, and just before she pitched into the crack between the boards, he brought her back with a flip of the token and the magic word.

He needed a safe place to put the token. Now that he knew it worked, he was scared he might lose it. It could fall out of his pocket when he was riding his bike or his mother could throw the box away by mistake when she did one of those cleaning raids on his room.

The castle. Of course. That's where it belonged anyway. He lifted one of the roof sections and tucked the cardboard box into a back corner in the master bedchamber. Mrs. Phillips's old room. That seemed right.

Downstairs he heard the hall clock ringing the quarter hour. He had to hurry. He only had fifteen minutes to get dressed and bike to the station.

Jason was standing on the cinder path looking up the tracks. William lay his bike down in the weeds by the side of the platform and tiptoed up behind him.

"Boo," he said in a low voice.

Jason jumped and then stamped his feet. "Blast, William, I hate it when you do that," he shouted. But he seemed embarrassed by his explosion. It showed how nervous he was, William thought.

"You're late," Jason muttered.

"Not by much," William said. "I was doing an experiment in the attic."

But Jason wasn't listening. "Is that the whistle?" he asked, cupping his hand to his ear. "The first one is supposed to come through at about eight-twenty."

"I don't hear anything," William said, but his heart flipped over.

"I brought your panniers," said Jason. "I thought we could go to the bike store afterward and exchange them."

"If there's an afterward," William said.

"Don't be stupid," said Jason, but William could see that he was scared too. He wanted to say, Hey, Jason, let's skip it. Let's just pretend we did it. Nobody else will know. It'll be our secret.

In the distance he heard the blow of the whistle. "That's it!" Jason cried. "Get ready," and before the words were out of his mouth, the freight train came around the corner.

The engineer blew his whistle again when he saw them. "Wave at him," Jason called. "As if we're just little boys excited about the train."

William and Jason jumped and waved. The engineer saluted them and blew his whistle again as he put on the brakes to slow down for the station. Suddenly the engine seemed to be on top of them, and it passed with a roaring rush of air that almost knocked William off his feet.

Jason looked over his shoulder as he started a long-legged lope beside the moving train. "The first boxcar has two ladders, one at each end," he yelled. "I'll take the front one." William fell into step behind Jason, trying to keep as close to his friend as possible.

When Jason turned to check again, William saw a wild look on his friend's white face that scared him more than anything else. The train had slowed down, but still William thought it was going too fast. How could he swing his body up onto the ladder?

"Next car," Jason screamed, and this time William looked over his shoulder too.

He stumbled, caught himself, and turned again just in time to see Jason grab the ladder. For the longest time, the bottom half of Jason's body swung back and forth underneath him like a dead thing, and William kept running, kept screaming at his friend to let go. By the time Jason had finally managed to haul his legs up behind him, William had missed his own ladder.

He slowed down and looked again. There was another double ladder coming, six cars down the line. He would get that one. He stretched his legs and tried to find some rhythm, some way of matching the train's heartbeat with his own. Up ahead he could see Jason's swaying body silhouetted against the sky as he inched his way across the top of his boxcar. William glanced back and counted cars. Two to go. He felt as if he had been running for hours. His heart was pounding so hard he thought it might blow right out of his chest.

Now he was shoulder to shoulder with the train. The steel wheels that thumped and clattered over the rails just a few feet below his face seemed to have become a part of him.

William looked back one last time, saw the ladder, reached out his hands, grabbed. He had it for a moment. For a swift terrifying moment, he felt his body lift up off the ground, but then his hands began to slip and he let them. He couldn't do it. He didn't want to do it. It was a really stupid thing to do. At the last minute, he jumped as far away from the train as he could, but when he hit the ground, he began to roll back down toward the tracks. Sky, then rocks in his face, then sky again, and he finally stopped a foot from the tracks.

The train seemed to go on forever. He lay on the ground with his eyes closed, too scared to move away from the screech and rumble of the wheels, too scared to look up and see if Jason had made it, too scared to crawl to his feet and find his best friend on the opposite side of the tracks.

Maybe he should run away, jump up now while the train still separated them and get on his bike. Or maybe he could stay here on the ground and pretend he'd really been hurt. He put his hand up to his face. There was a bump on his forehead and a couple of gashes, but the blood around them was already drying.

With a final blast of hot cinder breath, the great roaring wall of the train was gone and the world settled back into place. William pulled himself to his feet and watched the back porch of the caboose as it shimmied its way up the line to Canada. There it went. The train he didn't jump.

He heard Jason first. From across the tracks, on the other side of the station, came the shrieking and whooping of a boy who had jumped the trains. William stood and waited. The noises of triumph grew closer and closer.

They saw each other at the same moment. Neither one of them spoke for what seemed like hours. Jason leaned over and dusted off his jeans. William pushed the hair out of his eyes. From now on, it will always be this way, he thought. Jason on one side of the world and me forever on the other.

"What happened?" Jason asked.

"I missed the first ladder because I was watching you," William answered with a shrug. "And then I couldn't hold on the second time. My hand slipped."

"It doesn't matter," Jason said. "You can try it again next week." But he wouldn't look at William. He started walking to the bikes and William followed him. There was a line running through his brain over and over again. First time's the only one that counts, first time's the only one that counts.

"You were great," William finally said. Each word felt like a marble that he had to spit out of his mouth.

"Going over the top was the worst part," Jason said, his voice excited again. "I thought there'd be something to hang onto up there. But there wasn't. Just me and the roof of the boxcar.'' William didn't answer.

"I'm going to the bike store to turn in those panniers. I need some new tubes. You want to come?"

"I can't," William said. He was getting an idea. "I have to do some stuff at home. Can you come by my house afterward?"

"I don't think so. Dad is meeting me. He wants us to try to break our record up Snake Mountain."

"I've got something really important to show you," William said. "It won't take long."

Jason gave him a queer look.

"It's the thing Mrs. Phillips sent me for my birthday. It does something special. I want to show you how it works."

"Whaddya mean, something special?" Jason asked, settling his helmet into place. "It's just a little button."

William hesitated. He couldn't say magic. It was a stupid, baby word. Jason was already giving him a funny look, a look that seemed to say, Hey, listen, I jumped the trains, I'm a busy man, don't bother me.

"Just promise me you'll come," William said. "Promise me," he said again, and he knew his voice sounded desperate.

Jason shrugged. "Sure. No big deal, okay. I have to bring you the new panniers anyway." He flipped one long leg over the bike seat and settled himself into place. "See you," he said.

William waited until he had disappeared around the corner. Then he got on his own bike and pedaled as quickly as he could away from the tracks.

CHAPTER 4

As soon as he got home, William went looking for the neighbor's big gray cat. He found her in her usual place under their front porch.

"Here, kitty, kitty," he called in a soft singsong voice. "Come on out."

She crept cautiously forward until he could sweep her into his arms. He was halfway up the attic steps when his mother called from below.

"William, where are you? Jason's here."

"In the attic," he shouted back. "Tell him to come on up."

"They didn't have baskets for racing bikes," Jason said in a loud voice as he tromped up the last set of stairs. "I got you a tool kit instead. I left it by your bike."

"Great."

"I can't stay too long. Dad's going to be waiting for me."

"William," his mother called again, this time from the bottom of the attic steps. "I'm going to town. I've left a big pot of soup on the stove. I want you to turn it off in an hour if I'm not back."

"Yes, Mom."

She started up the steps, and William slipped the cat into Jason's arms and stepped in front of him.

"Listen, while you're up here, you might check for holes."

"Holes?" William said.

"I think there are mice or rats in the attic. Your father says I'm nuts, but I hear some animal scrabbling around up there at night. Look around, will you? Particularly down at the end that's over our bedroom."

"Okay, Mom." Maybe we should get a cat of our own, he thought to himself.

"Remember the soup," she said.

"Sure, Mom," he said, and finally she left.

Jason was still carrying the cat as he walked around the castle.

"I'd forgotten about this thing," he said. "It's pretty amazing. Mrs. Phillips gave it to you, didn't she?"

"That's right." William lifted the roof section and

felt around in the back of the bedchamber for the to-ken. His fingers found the cardboard box, and he drew it out carefully.

"Put the cat down in the middle of the courtyard," William said. "I need her to be trapped in one place. That way we'll be able to find her afterward."

"What are you going to do to her?" Jason asked.

"You'll see. Don't worry. It won't hurt her."

Jason lowered the cat, and in the small square of the courtyard, she turned around and around, sniffing the walls and poking her nose into the miniature door-ways.

"Okay, now get out of my way," William said as he held out the token. "I don't want to zap you too by mistake."

"I wish you'd tell me what you're talking about," Jason said as he took one step to the side.

"Janus," William said in a loud clear voice.

"Where'd she go?" Jason asked.

"She's right here." He scooped the little animal up from her corner by the kitchen and cupped his hands around her. "Come see."

Jason gave him a wary look.

"Come on," William said. "She won't bite." The cat's tiny paws tickled the skin on his palms. He opened his hands just wide enough for Jason to see inside.

"I don't believe this," Jason whispered. "She's still alive?"

"Sure."

"This is really weird. How'd you do it?"

"Magic," said William.

"Right," Jason said. "Magic. Did you give her some pill or something?"

"Nope. It's this token, the little button Mrs. Phillips sent me for my birthday. One side of it shrinks things, the other side makes them big again. Go ahead, you can touch her."

Jason hesitated. Finally he poked one finger inside William's hands and stroked the cat gently between its ears.

"This is the same cat that tried to jump Mrs. Phillips two years ago," William said.

"Mrs. Phillips?" Jason asked.

"I zapped her with the token out on the sidewalk so she couldn't leave for England, and this cat almost ate her."

"You did this to Mrs. Phillips?" Jason asked. "Made her this small?"

"Yes," William said. "She lived up here in the castle for a week."

"What did she eat?"

"I brought her stuff. And Sir Simon kept roasting mice for her on the spit, but I don't think she ever ate any."

"Sir Simon?"

William looked at his friend. He wondered how much he could take of this story at once. "Here," he said. "Put the cat back in the courtyard so I can zap her back to normal size."

"I want to do it," said Jason. Their eyes met. "Don't worry, I'll be careful," he said. "How do I do it?"

William showed him how to hold the token with the god's smiling face pointing out. "You say the word J-A-N-U-S. I'm spelling it because you don't want to say it until you're ready. Make sure I'm out of the way."

"You mean I could zap you?" Jason asked.

"That's right." William wished he could take the token back from his friend.

Suddenly Jason swung around and pointed it at a chair.

"Janus," he said loudly. Nothing happened.

"It only works on living things," William said quietly. "I'll do it, Jason."

"No, go on," Jason said. "Put her back in the courtyard. I'll do it right this time. I promise."

William released the tiny cat and snatched his hand away. Jason said the word, and suddenly the cat was bumping into the walls of the castle again.

"Amazing," Jason said. He pulled his glasses down and peered at the token.

"Okay, I'd better put it away," William said.

"Who is J-A-N-U-S?"

"The god who looks both ways in time. The month of January is named after him because he looks back at the old year and forward to the year to come." William held out the box with the lid off. He was itching to grab the token. Suddenly it scared him that Jason knew about it. Now that Jason had jumped the trains, William wasn't sure of him anymore. "Hey, Jason," he said, trying to sound casual. "I need it back."

After another long look, Jason dropped the little medallion into its bed of cotton. William slipped the top on the box and stuffed it into his pocket.

"That is one powerful little item," Jason said.

"I told you."

"Now who's this Sir Simon? Did he really catch mice and roast them?"

"It's a long story," William said. And now I wonder if I want to tell you, he thought. "You probably don't have time now. I mean, what about your father?"

"He's always late anyway. Just hurry up and tell me."

The cat suddenly jumped over the wall of the castle and disappeared behind one of the trunks.

"Can she get out anywhere?" Jason asked.

"No, leave her alone. Maybe she'll find those mice

Mom's talking about.'' William pulled over an old wooden box for Jason to sit on and a chair for himself. ''I'll try to keep this short. Remember when Mrs. Phillips gave me this castle as a going-away present?''

Jason nodded.

''Well, she gave me one lead knight with the castle. His name was Sir Simon.''

''How did you know his name?''

''He told me. He came alive in my hand the first time I picked him up.''

''Of course,'' Jason said with a grin.

''Look, I was right about the token, wasn't I?'' William said.

''I guess so. I mean I keep trying to figure if there's some trick to it.''

''Go ahead, figure away. What? I grab the real cat and throw a little one into the courtyard. Where am I going to find a miniature cat anyway?''

''Okay, okay,'' Jason said, putting up his hands. ''Don't get so crazy.''

William ran through the rest of the story as fast as he could. He told about shrinking Mrs. Phillips after Sir Simon came alive and the journey he took through the forest to Sir Simon's castle to help reclaim his kingdom from Alastor, the evil wizard who turned people to lead.

''I was the one who got Alastor in the end,'' William

said. He liked telling Jason that part of the story. "I knocked him over with a tumbling run."

But Jason was thinking of something else. "Didn't anybody miss you guys while you were gone?"

"That's the weird thing," William said. "If you go because you want to go, time stops in your world."

"But Mrs. Phillips didn't want to go. You did it to her."

"I know," William said with a sigh. "She lost that first week. She said she didn't mind. It made her feel younger."

For a while it was so quiet in the attic that William could hear the car horns on Riveredge Lane. He snuck a look at his friend. Any minute now Jason would check his watch.

"Hey, Jason," William said quietly. "We could go back."

"What do you mean?"

"I could zap you and you could zap me. We could go see them all. Sir Simon, Tolliver, the whole gang."

Jason stared at him. "Do you think it would work?"

"Why not? It worked last time. And the token's still doing its thing."

Jason finally did look at his watch. "Jeez, I've got to go. Dad's going to be really mad. He thinks I've been goofing off lately." He stood up, but he didn't move.

"We could take our bikes," William said.

"But it didn't work on the chair."

"It would work if we were sitting on them. I was wearing my backpack last time and it shrank along with me. And once we got to Sir Simon's, you could train for as long as you wanted."

"What do you mean?"

"Don't you get it? Time stops for you here, right?" William said. "So you could get in hours and hours of training that your father wouldn't ever know about. He'd be completely blown away when you got back. You could be *his* coach."

Jason sat down again with a bump. "You're right," he said. "I never thought about it that way. You sure nobody would know we were gone? And we'd get back at the same time we left?"

William shrugged. "That's what happened last time. When I walked downstairs with Mrs. Phillips, the clock said four-fifteen. Same minute on the same day that I left."

"That's too bad," Jason said with a grin. "There are a couple of tests coming up I'd just as soon skip."

"Me too," William said. "And a gymnastics meet."

"We'd have to pack some extra food and stuff," Jason said. "I'm definitely not eating any mice. And my tool kit and my stopwatch. We'll have to make a list."

William grinned. Good old Jason. He loved to make lists.

"All right!" Jason shouted and punched the air with his fist. "Wouldn't Dad be psyched if I came back with bulging muscles and a one-minute mile?"

Something crashed in the back of the attic and they both jumped at the noise.

"What was that?" Jason asked.

"Alastor," William whispered in a low, threatening voice. "The evil wizard has returned."

"Hey, cut it out," Jason said. "It's just the cat. This place is giving me the creeps."

"You find the cat while I hide the token."

"Here, kitty, kitty," Jason called in a low pleading voice as he crept back into the darkest corner of the attic. "No more shrinking. We promise."

William slipped the token into its box and this time he hid it in the armory. It wasn't that he didn't trust Jason. It was just that he wanted to be the only one who knew where it was. At least for now.

"Hey," Jason called. "I think your mother was right. The cat's sitting in front of a hole, swishing her tail back and forth."

"William, are you up there?" his mother called from the bottom of the steps.

"We're coming, Mom."

"You forgot to turn down that soup, William. It burned."

"Oh, gosh, sorry." He put his finger to his lips

when Jason reappeared with the cat cradled in his arms. "I forgot."

"William, I could kill you. I knew you weren't listening to me. You never do."

"You know, Jason found a hole up here in the baseboard. Looks like we got mice or rats or something."

"I told your father that I heard scratching noises up there. But he doesn't listen to me either. The two of you are just the same," she said, stomping down the back hallway.

"We definitely need to get out of here," William said with a grin.

"Are you sure we can get back?" Jason asked. "I mean there's no way we'd get stuck in Sir Simon's time?"

"Not as long as we have the token," William said. "You changing your mind?"

"Nope," Jason said in a firm voice. The cat began to squirm in his arms and he tightened his hold on her. "When do you want to go?"

"Next Thursday," William said. "After school."

CHAPTER 5

William had his bike halfway up the attic steps when he heard the kitchen door slam. Good. Jason could help him. William had already brought up his backpack filled with food and the binoculars and a flashlight, but the bike was a real pain. The stupid handlebars kept swinging around and hitting him in the chin, and twice the pedal had gotten hooked in the handle of a bucket sitting on the stairs.

"Jason?" he called.

"William."

Blast. It was his father. Why was he home so early? William's mind raced. He'd told the coach he was sick. Maybe she'd called his father's office.

"William, where are you?" his father called again. It sounded as if he were still down in the kitchen.

The bike was getting heavier by the minute. William couldn't stand on the steps forever.

"Nowhere, Dad. Not home. Go away," he whispered. "Please." He heard his father's footsteps coming up the stairs toward the attic door.

William was trapped, halfway up and halfway down. The door opened and his father's face appeared at the bottom of the steps.

"Hi, Dad," William said lamely. "What are you doing home so early?"

"I was checking on a construction site near the gym so I stopped by to watch your practice. Coach said you'd gone home with a headache."

William felt like melting through the floor.

"How're you feeling?"

"Much better," William said.

"It looks that way. It also looks like you could use some help here."

"That's okay, Dad. I've almost got it."

William bent his knees, hoisted the bike to his shoulder, and dragged it up one more step.

"I'll take the back half," said his father.

He lifted the rear wheel so quickly that William stumbled up the steps and almost fell into the courtyard of the castle.

"That's great, Dad. Thanks. Jason's coming over. He's going to teach me some basic maintenance. You know, greasing the hubs and stuff."

"Seems like the garage would be a better place to do that," said his father as he got down on his hands and knees and peered through the main gateway of the castle.

"Yeah, well, we thought—"

"Remember when I built the moat for this?" his father asked.

"Yeah, Dad, it's great." Phew, William thought, let's talk about moats.

"Mind if I raise the drawbridge?"

"No." William knelt beside him. "Help yourself. You know I don't really play with this castle anymore. I'm too old for it now. After all, I turned twelve last week."

"Twelve is twelve."

What does that mean? William thought. But his father didn't explain. He seemed to be concentrating on the miniature lever that raised and lowered the drawbridge.

"Twelve is too old to play with stuff like this," William said.

His father pinched the tiny chain between his thumb and forefinger and slowly raised the portcullis. "Twelve is too old and forty-two is just the right age," he said with a grin. "Where's that one knight you used to have?"

"He's gone," William said. "He marched off one day to do battle against an evil wizard."

"Did he win?"

"Yes. With a little help from a friend."

William glanced at his father. They often had these weird, sideways conversations. Why aren't you like Jason's father? he wanted to say. Why don't you coach me in something?

"Dad, I'm going to quit gymnastics soon. I'm sick of it. Why did you make me do it in the first place? It's a wimpy sport."

"Did I make you do it?" his father asked. "I don't remember that. You and Mrs. Phillips came up with the idea because you were small and wiry the way a gymnast is supposed to be. You still are."

"I don't like it," William said. "I'm too short."

"For what?"

"For anything. Basketball. Jumping. Life."

His father lifted one roof section, peered around, and set it back in place. "I never heard of anybody being too short for life," he said thoughtfully.

William groaned. His father didn't even argue right. He always got off the point. He should say things like, "Son, I don't care what you say, I want you to do such and such," and "Don't you speak to me like that, son, or you'll be in big trouble." That's what Jason's father would say.

"I hear somebody downstairs," his father said. "You don't suppose it's Jason do you?"

"I guess so," William said.

"He's making a terrible racket."

When William got downstairs, he found Jason with his bike halfway up the kitchen steps. He was swearing and muttering under his breath.

"You should have used the front staircase," William said as he clattered down to help him. "That's what I did. It's wider."

"The stupid pedal keeps whacking me in the leg. Now that I'm up this far, I'm not going down again."

William took the handlebars and backed up the steps while Jason wrestled with the bottom half of the bike. William's father met them in the upstairs hallway.

"Oh, gee, hi, Mr. Lawrence," Jason said, shooting a look of surprise at William.

"Hello, Jason. Perhaps you two should consider starting a bicycle-moving business. Of course I don't know if you'd find enough people who'd be interested in having their bicycles hauled around their houses." He held open the attic door. "However, it's a possibility. You know, in the winter. Boys, take my bike up to the attic, will you? Now that it's snowing, I think it's time to put it up on blocks."

"Hey, Dad."

"Yes, William?"

"You're talking a lot."

"Yes, William."

As the boys made their way up to the attic, Mr.

Lawrence watched from below. "I'm going to head back to work. See you later, boys."

"Yeah," William said. "Bye, Dad." As he watched his father's back disappear, he had a sudden urge to run after him and clap him on the shoulder or something. Just for a minute. Just when he remembered he wouldn't be seeing him for a while. But he didn't do it. Jason was watching.

"Your father's weird," Jason said.

"I know. But at least he didn't hassle us about the bikes. My mother would have killed me."

"Yeah, mine too." Jason moved his bike over so that it faced the castle entrance. "I've got to go down and get the rest of my stuff."

"What stuff?" William asked.

"My bike gear. And some food. I'm not taking any chances. Roasted mice or fried bugs are not good for muscle building."

"Lots of protein," William called after him.

When Jason came back, he was loaded down with both panniers and a backpack.

"Hey, Jason, that's too much stuff. You don't need all that."

"I sure do. Look, I'll show you." He opened the backpack and turned it upside down on the floor. "This handy little kit's got a spoke wrench and a six-piece hex wrench set. Dad just got it for me. Then I brought a pump and a spare tube, extra cables, spokes, and a chain tool.'' As Jason described each item, he held it up for William to look at. William groaned. At this rate they'd never get out of the attic.

"And gel gloves," Jason went on. "They're great for long distance. Your hands don't get sore. And my stopwatch."

William put up his hands. "All right, enough. I give up. I just hope the token works with all these things. Last time it was just me and the backpack."

"You mean the token has a weight limit the way they do on airplanes?" Jason asked. He grinned.

"I don't know." William shrugged. "Maybe it'll get worn out and lose its power. Then it won't be able to bring us back again."

"You worry too much," Jason said. They glared at each other. William was the first to look away. They hadn't talked about the trains. The news had spread at school that William hadn't jumped them. Nobody said anything, but all week he felt as if the other kids were looking at him and whispering behind his back.

"I'm not worried," William said in a loud voice. "But I brought practical things like a flashlight and matches and binoculars and peanut butter. And some chicken for dinner. Hope my mother doesn't notice it's gone."

"Okay, how do we do this?" Jason asked.

"I'll zap you first. Then I'll hand you the token and you do it to me. My father has already lowered the drawbridge. Let's get moving before somebody else decides to come home from the office."

Jason hooked on the panniers, put on his helmet and his backpack, and then walked his bike up to the edge of the moat.

William took the token from its hiding place and held it out. "You ready?" he asked.

"I guess so. Have I got everything?"

William smiled. "It looks that way. Unless of course you want to take the attic along with you."

William pointed the frowning face of Janus at his friend and said the god's name in a clear sharp voice.

He knelt next to the tiny figure waving up at him and flattened his hand against the floor. Jason pushed his bike up the edge of William's palm and along one of the creases.

"You feeling okay?" William asked quietly.

"It was really weird," Jason called through his cupped palms. "Like this big wind blowing around my face. How do I look? Have I still got everything?" He bent first one knee and then the other. "My legs still work," he said.

"Great. Hold on." William lifted his friend and then lowered him onto the drawbridge. "Now you can get off," he said. Jason rode his bike over the small hill of William's flesh. The bike tires tickled. "Here's the token," William said. "Wait until I've got my backpack on and I give you the thumbs-up sign."

Jason held his bike between his knees and took the token.

"Ready?" he called with one hand outstretched.

William nodded. He didn't even hear Jason say the word. He just felt the breeze lifting the hair off his forehead and a strange trembling in the air around him.

When he and Jason met in the middle of the draw-bridge, they gave each other two high fives, first with their right hands and then with their left. Before they wheeled their bikes across the drawbridge, William took the token from Jason and stuffed it safely away in his backpack.

CHAPTER 6

"I don't believe this," Jason said from the middle of the courtyard after they'd raised the drawbridge. "The castle feels so real. But where is everybody? Sir Simon and all the soldiers?"

"In his own castle," William explained. "On the other side of the forest. Remember I told you? We'll go there tomorrow."

"It's confusing."

"I know," said William. "Come on. We'll park our bikes in the stable, and I'll give you a tour."

"At least our horses don't need any hay," Jason said as he propped his bike against the rough wooden wall of the first stall.

"This is the armory," William said when they passed the first entrance beyond the stable. Jason tried to make a detour, but William steered him across the courtyard. Jason liked uniforms. Once he got in the armory, William knew he'd never leave.

He showed Jason the huge fireplace in the kitchen and the small side ovens where the bread was baked and then took him through the buttery and the covered passageway into the great hall.

"Jeez," Jason said as he stared up at the banners in the minstrel's gallery. "You don't see any of this stuff from the outside, do you?"

William didn't answer. He was amazed at how quickly everything was coming back to him. The castle walls, the layout of the rooms, the smooth, cold, stone floors. He led Jason up the stone steps in the tower to Mrs. Phillips's bedchamber. Every inch of the room seemed so familiar that he felt as if he had been there just the day before and she would be waiting for him in the corner, looking up from her needlework. But of course she wasn't. The only sign that she had ever been there were her surplice and tunic still hanging in the wardrobe.

"So who slept here?" Jason asked. "Sir Simon?"

"No. He slept outdoors, in the courtyard. This was Mrs. Phillips's room, the master chamber. I spent the night here before Sir Simon and I left. On the floor in front of the fire."

Jason wrinkled up his nose and sniffed. "Funny,"

he said. "It smells like her. Perfume or something."

So he smells it too, William thought. "Soap," he muttered. "She always used lavender soap. Come on," he said. "I'll show you the allure."

"Sounds like another kind of perfume," said Jason.

"It's the wall walk. In the old days, the guards used to stand up there and pour boiling oil on their enemies."

As they made their way along the walk, Jason ran his hand over the thick stones. "Pretty safe place," he said. He boosted himself up and hung out over the wall. "No enemies here," Jason said. "But I can't see the attic anymore either."

"That happens," William said. "You keep wondering where it's gone. And tomorrow when we go over the drawbridge, we'll walk right into the forest. At least that's what happened last time. Let's go down. It's getting dark. I need to start the fire."

"What's for supper, Mom?"

William grinned. "Chicken. It's already cooked but I'll heat it up on the roasting spit. You'd better eat a lot because after the chicken's gone, there's only peanut butter and jelly and fruit until we get to Sir Simon's."

"I brought protein bars."

"Good," said William. "After we finish them, it's roasted mice. Or rats. Dad thinks that hole you found is big enough for a rat."

Jason made a gagging noise and pretended to throw up over the edge of the wall.

"That'll probably work better than boiling oil," William said as he led the way down.

After dinner, they unrolled their sleeping bags in the courtyard.

"This is the life, William, old buddy," Jason said. "Food, drink, no parents around to bug us, no science report due tomorrow."

"Let's see. No forks or napkins. They didn't use them in the olden days," William said.

"No piano recitals," said Jason.

"No gymnastics meets."

"All the training time in the world," Jason went on. "I think we should take a vacation like this every month. If things get bad, we head up here for a little break."

William smiled. No trains to jump, he thought. But he didn't say it.

"It's hard to believe this is really happening," Jason said. He pulled the sleeping bag up around him as if he were putting on a pair of pants. "Maybe it's just a dream that we're both having at the same time."

"Sometimes with magic, you don't try to figure things out," William said. "It doesn't get you anywhere. Like right now, when you look up, what are you seeing? The attic ceiling or the sky?"

"The sky," Jason said. "I see stars."

"Where?" William asked. He followed Jason's pointing finger, and for a moment he thought he saw a twinkling light, but then it was gone. "Maybe," he said after a long moment. "Maybe."

He put his hands behind his head and wished for a pillow. Even though they'd carried the straw pallets down from the bedchambers, the floor of the courtyard felt hard. He shoved his backpack under his head. Lumpy, he thought, but better than nothing.

William could tell from his friend's steady breathing that he was already asleep. Jason slept the way he did everything else. Completely.

William didn't remember falling asleep himself. But when he opened his eyes and it was still dark, he knew he must have dozed off. His back felt stiff and cramped and something had woken him. Some noise.

"Jason, wake up," he hissed. "Do you hear that?"

"What do you want?" Jason groaned. "It's the middle of the night."

"Listen. Do you hear that noise? Like something gnawing."

Jason sat bolt upright as if he remembered suddenly where they were. "What is it?" he cried in alarm.

"I don't know," William said. "It's coming from the other side of the wall. Let's go look. I've got the flashlight."

Jason kept close behind, stumbling once or twice over the heels of William's running shoes as he tried to see ahead of them.

"I wish you'd remembered to bring a flashlight," William whispered.

"Yeah, me too," Jason grunted.

"Well, hang onto me while we go up the steps. I don't want you to trip over me." William felt Jason's fingers slip through his belt loop.

Like blind people, they slowly felt their way up the staircase inside the north tower. When they reached the top, William raised his hand. "Wait," he whispered. "Listen."

For a moment, they heard nothing. And then the same faint scratching floated up to them, this time from the direction of the south tower. They tiptoed along the walk until they stood right above the strange noise.

William shone the light over the side of the wall and it came to rest on the glossy dark fur of an animal.

"What is *that?*" Jason whispered. He was holding onto the sides of his glasses and staring through them as if they were binoculars.

"It's too big for a mouse," William said. "Gross. It's a rat. This must be what Mom was hearing."

At the noise above, the rat hesitated. Then it started its restless exploring again, this time up the wall with its paws. "It's climbing up," Jason said, his voice rising in panic. "It's going to come over the wall."

"Don't be dumb," William answered. "It's not big enough."

But when the rat had stretched to its full length, it was only a foot or two beneath them.

"It's not small like us," Jason said. "It's regular size. Where's the token? We'll zap it."

"Down in my backpack," William said quietly.

"Blast."

Suddenly William pointed the flashlight directly into the animal's eyes, flicked it off and then on again. The rat froze, blinded for an instant. Then it dropped to all fours and scrambled away.

"There," he said. "It's gone. For now."

"Where *is* your backpack?" Jason asked as they slid into their sleeping bags. "Just in case."

"Right here," William said. "Under my head."

They didn't speak for a long time, but neither one of them was asleep. William could hear Jason flopping around in his sleeping bag.

"William?"

"Mmm?"

"You know, I don't like surprises. It freaks me out when things jump on me out of nowhere."

"I remember," William said.

"So you really think the rat can't get in?"

"It's not tall enough to come over the wall. You saw."

"What if it tunneled under?"

"We'd hear it."

"Yeah," Jason said with a sigh. "I guess so."

Finally, he stopped stirring around.

When William opened his eyes the next morning, Jason was doing push-ups on the courtyard floor.

William stretched. He was glad to see daylight. "How'd you sleep? No rats pouncing on you in the middle of the night?"

"Nope," Jason said briskly. "But let's not hang around here all morning."

While William made breakfast, Jason checked his equipment one more time, repacking the panniers. Then he cleaned the chain and adjusted the brakes and the gears, chatting away at William about this part and that wrench. For once William was happy for Jason's patter. It kept him from listening for other noises.

Together they lowered the drawbridge.

Jason walked out first and peered around.

"See anything?" William called to him.

"Nope. Coast is clear."

William secured the drawbridge lever. "There won't

be anybody to raise this after we leave,'' he said. "No telling what will be roaming around in here when we get back.''

"Let's talk about something else,'' Jason said with a shiver. When William wheeled his bike up next to Jason, he noticed a lump under his friend's shirt.

"What's that?'' he asked.

Jason lifted his shirt. A dagger in its sheath hung from his belt.

"I found it in the armory,'' Jason said. "You've got the token. I need something to protect me too.''

"I knew you'd like that place,'' William said. "Just hide the dagger away somewhere so it's not as obvious.''

Jason slid it inside one of his panniers.

At the top of the drawbridge slope, Jason stopped and stared into the moat. "There's water in it,'' he cried. "Real water.''

William nodded. "I know. And look ahead. The path into the forest.''

"This is eerie,'' Jason said. "Nobody would believe this.''

"You're not going to tell them either,'' William said. "This is between us, remember.''

"I know,'' Jason said. He sounded for once as if he meant it.

William turned around. ''The legend has changed,''
he said. Jason read it out loud.

> *Two squires shall cross the drawbridge,*
> *Shall put themselves to the test.*
> *Knights know much of battle*
> *But the maiden knows the rest.*

''What maiden?'' Jason asked. ''Was there a maiden
last time?''

''No. Only an old lady named Calendar.''

''Maybe the legend is wrong.''

''Remember what I told you about magic?'' William
said as he pushed off on his bike. ''You just don't ask
too many questions.''

''The path looks pretty solid,'' Jason said as he took
the lead. ''Your tires should work okay even though
they're thin.''

William let him go ahead. All along, the castle was
waiting for us, he thought, as the branches of the trees
closed over him. He wondered what lay ahead as he
steered his bike toward the firmer sections of the path.
When he stopped to look back, the castle had disappeared.

CHAPTER 7

Jason set the pace, and for the early part of the morning, William didn't try to keep up. He pedaled along slowly. It was spring and the trees were buzzing with small birds that shrieked and twittered and darted from one fuzzy green branch to the next. Above the babble of the songbirds, he heard the occasional raucous call of a crow that seemed to say, Oh, be quiet, all of you.

Jason seemed to like sprinting ahead and then dropping back to lecture William on endurance or to tell him what he'd seen on the path. Most of all he seemed relieved to be away from the castle.

"Do you know why so many famous long-distance bicyclists have such spindly legs?" he asked William on one of his turnarounds.

"No," William said.

"Because they're not interested in thick muscles. They're interested in the blood that gets to those muscles. The more little veins that run into these babies," he said, leaning over and tapping his calf muscles, "the more oxygen they'll get and the farther they'll go. I read all about it this morning in my cycling magazine while you were snoring away."

Before William could respond, Jason sped away again, shoulders hunched, legs pumping. What would Sir Simon and Tolliver think of him? William wondered.

"It is the same forest, isn't it?" Jason asked the next time he circled back.

"I think so," William said. "Because of the bikes, we're making really good time, so we should see the river pretty soon."

"It's just ahead," Jason said. "Two more bends in the path."

When they got to the water, they left their bikes in the grass and clambered onto a flat rock. "This is where Sir Simon and I ate lunch," William explained.

"Lunch," said Jason. "What a great idea."

"It's only eleven o'clock."

"Who cares? I'm starving," said Jason as he began to unpack his pannier.

Jason munched his way through a bag of potato

chips, three peanut butter and jelly sandwiches, and two cans of juice before he showed any signs of slowing down.

"Anything else?" he asked hopefully.

William tossed him an apple.

"This is like feeding the animals in the zoo," he said.

When Jason finished the apple, he stood up. "Watch this," he said, hurling the core way out into the river.

"Maybe you shouldn't have done that," William said.

"Why not? It's biodegradable."

"It's funny, the river looks kind of dirty. It wasn't that way before." William pulled his binoculars out of his backpack and scanned the surface of the water. "There's all sorts of stuff floating down with the current."

"I don't see anything. What kind of stuff?" Jason asked.

"Stuff. I can't really tell what it is. There's a slimy trail on top of the water." He followed it up to the edge of the river. "And white things. Bones," he added in a low voice.

"Bones?" Jason asked. "You're kidding."

"See for yourself," William said, handing him the binoculars. "Over there. They've washed up on the shore where the river bends."

Jason shoved his glasses up into his hair. It took him a while to refocus the binoculars.

"This is creepy," he said. "I think they're animal bones, but it's hard to tell from here."

William took the binoculars back and looked again. "Some of them are pretty big for animal bones."

"We can't tell whose bones they are from this far away," Jason muttered. "I don't know about you but I don't plan to hang around and find out." He started to repack his pannier. William noticed he wasn't doing his usual methodical job but was shoving things in any which way.

"Don't worry, those bones aren't going anywhere," William said. "Maybe someone went hunting upriver and threw the stripped carcasses in the water. Remember they do things differently here."

Jason picked up William's backpack and his own pannier and headed back to the bikes. "I think they need a lecture on garbage collection."

William jumped off the rock into the sand. "Is that a boat out there?" he called to Jason.

"Who cares? Let's roll."

"No, wait, somebody's floating toward us on a log."

Jason went on tying his pannier to his bike. William watched as the strange figure drifted closer and closer to the shore.

"Hello," he called with a wave.

"What is that?" Jason asked as he came to stand beside William.

"It's a man," William said. "I think."

The log drifted in close enough so that the creature's feet touched the bottom. Then he flipped one enormously long leg over the log and stood up.

"See?" William said. "It's a man."

"He looks like a clown," Jason whispered.

The man was wearing an odd garment, a long-sleeved, purple jumpsuit that was held together in front by brightly colored ribbons. The wide pant legs were so wet that they clung to the man's flesh in dark wrinkled folds. When William looked closely, he could see that the dye from the material was turning the water purple.

"Lobelia petals," said the man whose curly gray hair stood out around his face like a fuzzy halo.

"Lobelia petals?" William repeated.

"Never can resist the color but the dye doesn't hold," the fellow said as if this explained everything.

Jason covered his mouth with his hand. "Be careful," he muttered to William. "He looks crazy."

The man did a little dance in the sand, perhaps to shake some of the extra water from his clothes. "Deegan's the name," he said with a bow so deep that his forehead banged right into his wet knees and came up again with a faint purple stain. "Honorary, temporary, roaming fool, court jester, and erstwhile magician to the leader of this fair land, the Right Honorable Sir Simon of Hargrave, otherwise known as the Silver Knight, my liege and master, though no fool serves a knight that does not make that knight foolish. For what purpose does a fool serve but to remind us of all the folly in the world?" He posed this question to them with such a serious frown on his stained forehead that William felt compelled to answer.

"Why, none, your honor, I mean, Sir Deegan. Except to make us laugh."

"Precisely. And no Sir about it, half-boy, half-man. Deegan will do. Or your foolship." And with no warning, he raised his arms and tilted over into a cartwheel which turned into another and another. He was spinning so fast that he looked like a huge purple pinwheel headed directly for them.

"Stop it," Jason cried. "Stop right there." William paid no attention to his friend. He was mesmerized by the purple circle rolling toward them, by the rubber man who had called him half-boy, half-man.

Jason muttered something else that William couldn't hear clearly, and then the creature was gone. He had melted into thin air.

"Where'd he go?" William asked.

Jason was stuffing something into the pocket of his shorts when William looked directly at him.

"Give it to me," William said. He was so angry he felt his throat closing up. The second time he screamed at Jason, louder than he had ever screamed at anybody. "GIVE IT TO ME!"

Jason backed off. "Okay, okay. Don't get so mad. This guy was coming straight for us. He could have hurt us."

"Now," William said in a low, threatening growl that surprised even him. He sounded like a chained dog.

Jason reached over and dropped the token and its box into William's palm.

"We've got to find him," William said. Slowly and carefully he lowered his body to the ground. "You'd better watch where you put your feet. Being buried alive in the sand would be a horrible way to die."

"Gee," Jason said, "I didn't think—"

"No," William said. "I guess you didn't." He was so angry with Jason that he couldn't look at him. He remembered the time he put a key chain down by his towel on the beach. One minute it was there, the next it was gone. He never found it again.

He used his eyes like minesweepers, back and forth, back and forth, across each minute grain, looking for a purple arm, the gray hair, anything that moved.

"Deegan," he called over and over again.

Jason had lain down on his stomach on the rock. He hung over the edge, calling out the man's name in a soft, scared voice.

With every passing minute, William panicked a little more. His fingers were itching to start digging, but he knew how easily the sand shifted, how dangerous it would be for the miniature man if William chose the wrong spot. Even though they had only just met, Deegan seemed incredibly important to him all of a sudden.

"Do you see anything?" Jason asked.

William shook his head. But then he did. Out of the corner of his eye, he caught a hint of color. The small purple man had found a weed, one of those scrawny ones that grow directly out of the sand, and he was clinging to it. But whenever Deegan tried to put his feet down, the sand would give way and the leaf would dip and he'd bob up and down like a little kid on a trampoline.

"I see him," William whispered. "But we mustn't scare him. He's grabbed a weed under the shelter of the rock. We can't bring him back to normal size while he's under there. He has to come out first."

William inched closer and very carefully laid his open right palm in the sand.

"Deegan," he said quietly.

The man looked wildly around, still swinging on his leaf.

"He looks like Tarzan," said Jason, who was hanging upside down over the edge of the rock.

"You have to jump onto the palm of my hand," William explained. "Do you see it?"

The man nodded.

"Now I'm going to move it closer. Don't be scared. I'll be very careful. I promise."

"What have you done to me?" Deegan called.

"Jason will explain that in a minute," William said. He slid his palm along the sand until it rested right next to the stem of Deegan's weed. "There now," William said. "Jump."

Deegan eyed him warily. "I don't blame you if you don't want to trust us," William said. "But you don't have much choice right now." Out of the corner of his eye, he saw a beetle making its dainty way across the sand toward the little man. Deegan spied it at the same moment and tried to scramble frantically up the swaying leaf.

"Jason," William said in a quiet voice. "Do you see the beetle headed our way? Get rid of it, will you?"

Jason dropped his hand like a wall between the beetle and the purple man so the insect changed direction abruptly and scuttled away into a dark crevice in the rock.

With that, Deegan finally let go of his leaf and dropped onto William's palm.

"Better sit down," William said. "My hand isn't very steady." Deegan folded his legs and sat in a cross-legged position, looking like a stern little Buddha. William carried him carefully up to the rock.

"Now, stand there without moving," William explained once Deegan had crawled off his palm. "We'll have you back to your regular size in a second."

Just as William held out the token, Jason stopped him.

"Can I do it?" he asked. They looked at each other.

"Please," Jason begged. "I promise I won't mess around this time."

"All right," William said at last.

Jason knelt down, pointed the token, and said the magic word. In no time at all, Deegan was towering over them.

"Gee," Jason said. "You're tall."

"Tall, yes, but hardly powerful enough against your magic. May I see it?" he asked, holding out his long arm.

Jason glanced at William who nodded his agreement. For some reason which he couldn't explain even to himself, William trusted this strange purple man.

"And where did you procure this dangerous little medallion?" Deegan asked as he turned it over in his own palm.

"From Alastor, an evil wizard who used to rule over this land."

"And how does it work?"

William explained the symbolism of the two sides of the token.

"Janus who guards the gates of time," Deegan said after he handed the token back to William. "Now may I know your names?"

Jason was still eyeing Deegan warily. He looked like a cat ready to pounce.

"Remember, Boy Who Looks through Windows," said Deegan, his head to one side, "a fool does not fight. That's the job of the king and the knight and the noble warrior as you yourself appear to be."

"These things are called glasses," Jason said as he pushed them back up on his nose. "And my name is Jason Stubbs Hardy." Then he drew himself up to his full height. In normal circumstances this was considerable, but, next to this long-legged, purple-garbed man, he didn't look very big anymore. And I must look like a shrimp, William thought.

"I am William Edward Lawrence," William said.

"William and Jason. Noble names, I believe. Of distinctive lineage. You have come to see my lord, perhaps to challenge him to some silly jousting tournament with those peculiar steeds of yours. They are no doubt resting for the fight now."

He was referring to the bicycles which lay in cock-eyed positions in the grass where the boys had dropped them. Jason giggled. "They're not the ones who need resting," he said. "We do."

"We've come to visit Sir Simon. He's a friend of mine," William said. "Is he all right?"

"In fine fettle," said Deegan. "Right pleased with himself, I'd say. Always is when he's off to a fight."

"A fight?" asked William. "Not another one."

"Oh, so you do know his penchant for his sword. Dear Sir Simon. Always upholding the name of Hargrave. Such a tiresome task it seems to me, as it will never be finished." Deegan dropped backward in what looked like a back walkover, but he ended up with his face curling around and looking up at them from between his calves. "Like this, a circle," he said with an apologetic smile. "Never finished. Round and round."

"You sure are flexible," Jason said. "I mean for such a tall person."

William wished the fool would uncurl himself. Talking to a head which was resting in a place where it wasn't supposed to be made him feel sick to his stomach.

Deegan put his hands down, and with one swift movement, flipped his body over itself and stood up.

"Who will he be fighting this time?" William asked.

"Merely practice. A jousting tournament in a neighboring kingdom," said Deegan. "The winter was cold and dreary and Sir Simon has been cooped up in the castle for too long. He fairly itches for travel and adventure.''

"Who will guard the kingdom while he's gone?''

"Dick and young Tolliver and Gudrin. And you two, I expect. That's probably why you're here.''

"How about you?'' Jason asked.

"I shall accompany my noble lord. No proper knight goes jousting without his fool in the hopes that he shall make some opponent appear foolish. I'm rather looking forward to it. There shall be a feast of fools and we shall have our own kind of joust. One trickster outdoing another.''

"Who's Gudrin?'' asked William.

"Tolliver's cousin, Dick's niece. We had a terrible plague of the milk sickness last year, and Dick's wife and her sister died on the same day.'' Deegan leaned over and picked two wet leaves from between his toes.

"Is Calendar still alive?''

"So many questions,'' Deegan said with a frown. "No, the poor soul. She was sent to live in a convent just the other side of the forest. With the Sisters of the Holy Cross. She died there not long ago. Some people say that at the end she had gone quite mad.''

"Mad?'' William asked.

"Crazy in the head, not right.'' Deegan tapped his own head with a skinny finger one, two, three times, like a woodpecker driving a hole into the bark of a tree.

And every time he tapped, his head moved a little more to the left until he ended up with one ear resting on his shoulder. "Foolish," he added, grinning at them from this sideways position.

Nobody said anything more until Jason broke the silence. "Time to get moving," he announced. "We want to make the castle by nightfall."

"Easily done," Deegan said with a shake of his shoulders. "I shall go along with you. I was sent to find Gudrin. She's been out in the fields hunting herbs for two days and Dick wants her home."

"If you keep your feet up, you might be able to ride on the handlebars," Jason said, picking up his bike.

"A kind offer, dear sir, but I think not." Deegan was eyeing the bicycle a little nervously, William thought.

"Go on ahead," William said to Jason. "I'll walk my bike for a while." Jason pushed off, obviously happy to be moving again.

Once they had gone a little way down the path, Deegan said, "You are *the* boy, aren't you?"

"You said half-man and half-boy," said William.

"True. But you are the boy from before. The one they speak about. Muggins. Legendary vanquisher of Alastor. The tumbling fool. The best disguise of all, in my opinion."

A little shiver of excitement ran down William's

back. So they hadn't forgotten. He was a legend. He wished Deegan had said this in front of Jason. "Yes," he said, trying to look modest but not feeling it one bit. "I am that boy."

"And are you still a tumbler?"

"Not as good as I used to be. I'm getting too old for it."

"Half-boy and half-man," said the fool again. "I never made it across from one side to the other. I shall tumble and fool my life away." He did a quick handstand. His bare dirty toes wiggled along in the air like upraised hands until he righted himself.

"So Tolliver and this Gudrin both lost their mothers and their grandmother in one year," William said slowly.

"It has not been an easy time," Deegan said. "And Dick's taken it the hardest of all. He has moments when he acts like his old self, but the losses in his family have aged him. I expect we shall be needing your help in the days to come." The fool's face grew quite serious.

"For what?"

The tall man shrugged. "Nobody knows precisely. Calendar tried to warn us before she died, but then visions are often mistaken for madness. That's why Sir Simon had her sent to the convent. Her 'fits,' as he called them, made him uneasy. But Gudrin believed her. And there have been signs. Omens. Portents.''

"Bones in the river," William said.

"Ah, I see you have sharp eyes."

"What other portents?"

"A ship blown in on an ill wind at high tide. Not a ship but a coffin with a cargo of skeletons." His voice dropped to a whisper. "Bones to hold the tiller and bones to hoist the sails. Not a pretty sight. But Sir Simon had it towed out to sea again and will hear no more about it, mind you. He says Gudrin is a young and foolish girl, and of course foolishness is my trade. A fool is put on this earth to make a body laugh. Sir Simon says my fooling has grown too serious of late. Perhaps he is right. Enough of this."

For a moment, William could think of nothing to say. The sun had slipped behind a cloud and the sudden breeze felt chilly.

He heard a shout from Jason in the distance.

"Go on," Deegan said. "I want to see you ride that silly contrivance. I'll catch up."

CHAPTER 8

By the time William caught up with Jason, he was standing by a wall talking to a skinny girl. She had straight hair that tumbled over her shoulders in tangled blond lumps. On her lap she held a basket filled with plants that looked as if they had just been pulled out of the ground. She stared at William as he pushed his bicycle through the tall grass toward her.

"You must be Gudrin," William said.

She nodded. "How do you know my name?"

"We met your friend Deegan in the forest. He's coming along behind. Your uncle wants you home."

"I do wish they would leave me be," she grumbled. "They should be paying more attention to roving visitors with peculiar metal horses."

Jason caught William's eye. "I tried to explain about the bikes," he said.

William turned back to Gudrin. "I have visited your land before," he said. "My name is William Edward Lawrence. Sir Simon is a good friend of mine."

The girl just kept on staring.

"Muggins," he added hopefully.

"Muggins yourself," she said, wrinkling up her nose as if something smelled bad. "Never heard of you."

"I played the fool Muggins. The one who defeated Alastor."

"I have heard tales about that time," she said. "But I didn't live in the castle then." She slid off the wall just as Deegan came trotting up.

"So you have met," he said.

"That we have," said Gudrin. "And I understand you've been sent to fetch me. I do tire of Uncle treating me like a child, Deegan."

"Sir Simon is leaving tomorrow," Deegan explained. "I expect Dick wishes to have you safe in the castle before then."

"Whatever for?" Gudrin asked, her voice sweetly syrupy. "According to him, there is no danger to be feared in our fair land." Her eyes narrowed. "Have you seen the bones?"

"Yes," he said. "I came down the river. It was not a pretty sight. Offal and bones."

"Something is amiss," she said. Her eyes slid around to William.

"We saw them too," William said quickly.

"Enough of this," she declared with a toss of her head. "I expect we should be off."

As usual Jason rode ahead. William walked his bike alongside Deegan and Gudrin, who had fallen into earnest conversation.

"William knew your grandmother well," Deegan said. "Tell him what she said."

"Can he be trusted?" Gudrin asked. "Will he think me mad?"

William didn't like them talking about him as if he weren't there. "Yes, I can be trusted and no, I won't think you mad. Calendar and I went through a lot together," he said. "Without her, I would never have known how to defeat the wizard."

"There," said Deegan. "An honest answer."

"Before she died, my grandmother tried to warn us of some terrible danger that was coming," Gudrin explained. "She said it would rise up and destroy us all, that it would be worse than anything we had seen before."

"What kind of danger?" William asked.

"It was hard to make sense of it," Gudrin said wearily. "Sometimes she spoke in riddles and at other times, quite plainly. Toward the end, when she saw that Deegan and I were the only two who believed her, she grew more desperate. In those days, she acted almost as if she were possessed by the devil himself. Her eyes would get huge and a high-pitched shrieking voice would come out of her mouth. That's when Sir Simon had her sent down to the convent.''

"What did she chant?"

Gudrin and Deegan exchanged a look.

"Do you remember it?" he asked.

"Of course," she said. Her voice sounded tired.

> *Come to ravage*
> *Come to kill*
> *Bones will crack*
> *Blood will spill*
>
> *Babies' cries*
> *Old men's eyes*
> *Nothing left*
> *To feed the flies.*
>
> *Evil lurking, evil rising*
> *Washed in with the tide*
> *Never satisfied*
> *Till we all have died.*

"But what is it?" William asked. All this mumbo-jumbo talk was giving him the creeps. "What are we supposed to be looking for?"

Gudrin shrugged. "Who knows? Nothing good, I warrant you that. And there have been signs lately that all is not right in the land. Sir Simon dismisses it as the prattlings of a foolish girl. Even when the ship came, he ignored it."

"Deegan told me about the ship," William said. He looked around but Deegan had disappeared. "Where did he go?"

"He comes and goes with no warning, to suit his pleasure," Gudrin said. "You never know where he'll turn up next." She shuddered as if to shake off the bad thoughts and changed the subject. "Don't you know how to mount that thing?"

"Sure I do."

"Well, you always seem to be pushing it along. At least my horse walks by himself."

"But you have to feed a horse. A bike doesn't eat anything. All you have to do is pedal it."

"Show me."

William got on his bike and coasted down the little hill in front of them. He waited at the bottom for her to catch up.

"Why doesn't it tip over?" she asked.

"Balance," he said. "You have to learn to balance it. You want to try?"

She handed him her basket and leaned over to tie up her skirts. By the time she was through, she had twisted the various layers of cloth into a garment that looked like an odd pair of very baggy pants. She reminded William of a small Persian sultan without the turban. He couldn't help smiling.

"So what's wrong with it?" she asked with her chin stuck out. "This is what I do when I go riding."

"Nothing," he said quickly. "You have to swing one of your legs over the bar. Like a horse."

Once she was on, William held the bike and showed her how to use the brakes and the pedals.

"Now I'll run along beside you for a while till you get the hang of it. It's hard to do. Most people start with training wheels when they're little kids."

"Come on," she said impatiently. "Stop talking and give me a push."

For her first time on a bike, she didn't do badly at all. She stayed upright for at least a minute after William let her go. But when the front wheel began to wobble, she tried to pedal faster and then tipped slowly to the left.

"Lean the other way!" he yelled, but she couldn't right herself in time. She went over with a shriek.

He pulled the bike off her.

"Are you all right?"

"Fine," she said, scrambling to her feet. "I want to try it again."

The next two times, she went a little farther before

she pitched over. She looked as if she were ready to go on practicing all day. At this rate, William thought, we'll never get to the castle.

Just then he heard a shout, and Jason rounded the corner with a boy on his handlebars.

"Is that Tolliver?" William asked.

"The very one," she said. "My little cousin."

"Little. He looks a lot bigger than I remember," said William.

"His legs have grown faster than his brain," she muttered.

When Jason braked, Tolliver jumped off and ran up to them.

"Sir William," he cried. "It *is* truly you. I did not believe it but now I see you with my own eyes."

"Tolliver, what happened to your legs?" William asked.

"What is wrong with them?" Tolliver said. He sounded worried.

"They've grown a considerable amount in my absence," William answered with a grin.

"Sir, you are funning me and that is not kind."

"Pardon me, *Sir* William," said Jason. "But what's been taking you so long? I've been halfway to the castle and back?"

"Progress has been slow," William said without looking at Gudrin.

"What he means is he's been teaching me to ride that contrivance," Gudrin said.

"Master Jason has promised to teach me to ride too, once we reach the castle," said Tolliver.

Jason shrugged. "Might as well. I can't have the boy on my handlebars all the time. Don't know what damage it may be doing to that front tire. What happened to Deegan?"

"He went off on his own," William said. "Sort of melted away actually. For the second time today."

Jason looked uncomfortable.

"Tolliver, what news of the castle?" Gudrin asked.

"All hustle and bustle. Sir Simon is making preparations for his journey," Tolliver said. "I have begged him to take me along but he will not allow it. Sir William, the word of your coming has reached the castle and Sir Simon sent me to meet you. Everybody is eagerly awaiting your arrival."

William's heart swelled. What would good old Jason think of that? "Well, then, let's be on our way," he said with a ceremonious wave of his hand. "We should reach the castle by late afternoon, Tolliver?"

"Yes. Or even sooner if we ride," Tolliver said with a gleam in his eye.

"Gudrin could ride on my handlebars," William said.

"They look too skinny. I'll fall off."

"So what?" he laughed. "That's what you've been doing anyway."

She tried not to laugh but it didn't work. "All right, Master William Muggins, prepare my seat."

They folded her herbs into one of the panniers and tied her basket to the other. Then William flipped the handlebars up and she clambered aboard. He pushed off three times before he built enough momentum to hold his balance. Her tangled blond hair blew into his eyes and tickled his face, but he did not dare lift his hand to brush it away. She smelled odd, musty and fresh at the same time, like a spade of earth newly turned over. From time to time, she cried out in excitement and leaned suddenly to one side, which meant William had to compensate by throwing his weight just as suddenly to the other.

As they drew closer to the castle, the people began to gather along the side of the road. Men came out of the fields to shout a greeting. From the doors of the houses, women waved and the children who clung to their thick skirts raised their hands too.

William and Gudrin caught up with Jason who was walking his bicycle between the rows of people.

"Where's Tolliver?" William asked as they wobbled to a stop. Gudrin clambered off and untied her skirts.

"He's gone ahead," Jason said. "To announce your

lordship's arrival,'' he added with a roll of his eyes.

Now some of the people were falling into step behind them and seemed intent on walking all the way to the castle, although they kept their distance from the bikes. It began to feel like a parade.

"What did you do with the wizard?" they called to William.

"He's gone forever," William called back.

"And you've brought some strange horses with you this time," said an old man, eyeing the bikes nervously.

"Sir Simon has sent for you, then," said a large woman with a baby on her hip.

William gave up trying to answer them all. He just smiled and waved and felt as if he were going to burst apart inside.

And all along the way, he heard them saying, "It's the boy. The boy's come back."

Jason shot William a look across the top of Gudrin's head. "The boy," he said. He seemed both impressed and skeptical at the same time.

"Half-boy, half-man." William was startled by Deegan's words tumbling out of his mouth without any warning. Gudrin, who had drawn closer to him as the people pressed around, gave him a queer and interested look but she said nothing.

"And this is my good friend who has journeyed with me a long distance," William called as he waved his hand in Jason's direction. "A brave and noble fellow."

The crowd cheered and clapped and a flush of color spread slowly over Jason's cheeks.

"Cut it out," he muttered, but he didn't look as if he meant it.

The castle loomed up above them on its rise. From each tower, brightly colored pennants curled lazily in and out on the passing breezes. Sir Simon was standing with a group of his guards on the wall walk, his hand raised in a salute of welcome. William put up his own right arm and kept it high as they drew closer and the drawbridge was slowly lowered to receive them. They took off their helmets and trundled the bicycles across the thick wooden planks. When Sir Simon appeared before them in the courtyard, William handed his bicycle to Gudrin. The buzz of the crowd faded away into silence as William walked forward into his old friend's outstretched arms. Back at home, he never hugged people. It didn't seem manly. But here with this big bear of a man, a hug seemed the only thing to do. They clapped one another on the back, parted, stared into each other's eyes, and hugged again. They were too choked with emotion to speak, and in the silence, people shuffled their feet and looked at the ground. Somewhere in the back of the crowd, a child cried out, and the sudden sound broke the spell.

"My boy," Sir Simon said at last. "You have returned."

"I have," said William.

"Alastor?"

"In the bottom of the ocean or so Mrs. Phillips reports."

"Mrs. Phillips?"

"The Lady Elinore to you, my lord," William teased.

"She is well?" asked Sir Simon.

"From all I hear tell. She lives with her brother now. She sent me the token for my twelfth birthday, so I decided to come back and see you." Suddenly he remembered Jason. "And I brought a friend. This is Jason, a fellow squire with strong legs and a keen eye."

"You are welcome, young man," Sir Simon said, putting on his lordly voice. "Any friend of William's has a place with us." The people clapped and cheered. Sir Simon raised his hand for silence. "Now, as you all know, I will be leaving tomorrow to make my way to the castle of the Lord of Babbingdale, Sir Edgar of Inglewich, for the great joust. As some of you will recall, your humble lord distinguished himself in the lists one year ago, and it is, of course, incumbent upon him to return and defend the honor of the name of Hargrave and our kingdom. Tonight many of our fellow knights will be joining us for a feast, and tomorrow morning there will be a celebration in the courtyard before I depart with my entourage. All are welcome.'' The people cheered again and then slowly began to disperse as Sir Simon beckoned to the travelers.

The guards pressed forward to greet them, and somewhere in the middle of the confusion, William noticed that Gudrin had slipped away. She came back some time later with her uncle. Dick seemed genuinely glad to see the boys. He smiled and even laughed when Tolliver told him stories of his ride on the handlebars. But William could see a difference in the man. Sadness had dropped over his face like a shade over a window. Gudrin stuck close by his side and was gentle and attentive.

The rest of the day passed in a tumult of greetings and feasting and exploring the castle. William and Jason were shown to the bedchamber next to Sir Simon's by Brian, the head guard.

''That man seemed to know you pretty well,'' Jason said.

''Yes. He was in charge of me when I was Alastor's prisoner. We became good friends.''

''It's a lot better than last night,'' Jason said as he looked around the tall stone room. ''More straw in the mattress—''

"Pallet," William said. "Mattresses haven't been invented yet."

"Whatever," Jason said, standing on his tiptoes to peer through the arrow loop. "I wish the windows weren't so skinny."

"They're built that way for defense. So we can see out to shoot arrows but the attackers have a hard time hitting us."

"Hey, teach, give me a break," Jason said. "Enough of the history lesson."

William didn't answer.

Jason set about unpacking his panniers. He laid his tools and magazines out in his usual methodical way. "So how long will Sir Simon be away? He sounds as if he wants us to run things around here but we can't stay forever."

"I guess we'll find out tonight at the feast," William said.

"The feast?" Jason groaned.

"Just close your eyes, hold your nose, and swallow."

CHAPTER 9

At the feast, William ate whatever was set in front of him. It all tasted perfectly okay, he decided, as long as he didn't know what it was. The boys were seated on either side of Sir Simon who filled the air with talk of the upcoming tournament and the knights he expected to meet in the lists.

"How long will you be gone?" Jason asked him at a break between courses.

"Three phases of the moon, perhaps a few days more," Sir Simon said. "That suits you?"

"Oh, yes, sir. Extra training time," he called to William above the noise.

"Training?" Sir Simon asked.

"On the bicycle. I'm building up my muscles for a long trip I have to take this summer—" Jason stopped.

"Well, this summer on the other side. You know, in our time."

Sir Simon nodded. "I know. Where the Lady Elinore lives. Tolliver seems quite excited about your bicycle. He says you have agreed to teach him how to ride it."

"Yes, sir. I could teach you too."

Sir Simon put his head back and roared with laughter. "I doubt I shall need a steed like yours, young Jason. My horse, Moonlight, and I do quite well together, thank you very much."

"Are you taking all the guards with you?" William asked.

"No. I shall leave your old friend, Brian, and a number of his trusted legion. And I have ordered extra guards posted at the border."

"Are you expecting trouble?" Jason asked.

"Heavens no, my dear boy," said Sir Simon. "But one must always be prepared. My spies have been out in the countryside, making their usual discreet inquiries. They have reported back to me that, except for the odd poacher, there is no danger to speak of."

"And what's this talk about a skeleton ship?" William asked.

"I see you've been listening to Gudrin," Sir Simon said. "She is nothing but a young slip of a girl. Like her grandmother, dear Calendar, she puts too much store in portents and visions."

"And Deegan?"

"Ah, yes, my fool. He has a good heart, you can be sure of that, but one never puts one's trust in a fool."

"The ship *was* in the harbor," William persisted.

"It was. But I had it towed out to sea and the current bore it away. With my own eyes, I watched it go." Sir Simon frowned and lowered his voice. "It would not be wise to talk any more of the ship. The common people are prone to superstitions and gossip spreads through the kingdom like water." He stood up. "Now come, my boys, it's off to bed with the two of you. I want you up bright and early. I wish you to take part in the celebration tomorrow in some small way."

"What do you mean?" Jason asked.

Sir Simon smiled and wagged his finger. "So curious, my boy. I like that. But the matter will wait till morning." He put an arm around each of them and crushed them against his thick body for a brief, painful moment. "I am off tomorrow," he said. "At long last."

As usual, Jason fell quickly into a deep sleep. William lay on the straw pallet and stared at the thin strip of moonlit sky through the arrow loop. He pulled the animal fur up to his chin. Even though the spring afternoons were warm, all the cold despair of winter days seemed to seep out of the stone walls of the castle during the night, and he felt it in his bones. The ship was gone, he told himself. Blown back to sea. Deegan was nothing but a fool and Gudrin a girl with a vivid imagination. Of course, his old friend, Sir Simon, wouldn't go off and leave them if there were any real danger.

The next morning the passageways of the castle swarmed with people preparing for the great departure. William and Jason stumbled from their chamber at the sound of shouting and spent the rest of the morning ducking out of the way. Every so often, they could hear Sir Simon belting out some new command from his bedchamber, and a nervous squire or a harried chambermaid would rush to carry out his wishes. Down in the kitchen, the scullion boys were busy packing provisions for the journey in large rush baskets while the cooks removed steaming loaves of fresh bread from the brick ovens. William slipped in and snatched some dried fruit and meat and a few hunks of bread when nobody was looking.

"I wouldn't mind two fried eggs and a plate of bacon and three pieces of toast with strawberry jam," Jason said as he gnawed on the dried figs. "These are as tough as my hiking boots and they don't taste much better."

"Let's go up to the wall walk," William said. "We'll be out of the way there."

From above, the courtyard looked like a train station at rush hour, with people scurrying in every direction, shouting at one another, then dropping bundles and hurrying to pick them up again. The clang of metal against metal rose above the tumult of human voices as the blacksmith completed his final repairs on the weapons Sir Simon was to take with him. In one corner of the courtyard, a man had set himself up as the local barber. He was doing a thriving business on the heads of various travelers. One by one, the horses were led up from the stables underneath the barracks into the sunlight of the inner courtyard. The pages groomed the mounts, saddled them, and then hung on them the brightly colored drapes that signified the procession to a tournament. The horses, sensing the excitement in the air, shifted about and stamped their feet.

"They look silly all dressed in skirts like that," Jason said. "Like a lot of ladies going to a party."

"See the biggest horse?" William said, pointing.

"The white one giving Tolliver all the trouble?"

"That's right. That's Moonlight, Sir Simon's stallion. It is a great honor for Tolliver to be dressing him. It means that Sir Simon has chosen him as his personal page. Next year, when Sir Simon rides out to a tournament, Tolliver will probably go with him."

"Lucky," Jason said quickly. He glanced at William and shrugged. "It'd be fun to try it once."

Brian marched up to William and saluted him. "If it will please you to accompany me, Sir William. And also your companion. Sir Simon desires your presence in his chamber."

"Very well, Brian." They fell into step beside him.

"We are honored by your visit, my lord," the soldier said.

"Thank you, Brian," William said. "I am glad you will be staying with us in the castle."

He grinned. "You and I, we have faced trouble before, have we not?"

"That we have," said William.

An hour later William and Jason stood behind the wall of the barracks waiting for a signal.

"This is a crazy idea," Jason said. "A boy on a bicycle dueling with a knight on a horse." He readjusted his helmet again. It was a little too big so that the visor fell down over his nose when he least expected it. "It's hot in here. My glasses keep fogging up," he babbled in William's ear. His voice sounded as if it were coming through a long tunnel. "How am I supposed to hold this lance and ride at the same time? And this chain mail shirt is itchy. I'm glad he didn't make me wear the full suit of armor. My poor bike would have been completely squashed under the weight."

"It's all for show," William reminded him for the fourth time. "You don't really have to knock the guy off. Sir Simon just wants to make a fool of Sir Morlan who played some trick on him last year. That's why he's making you hide back here. When the trumpets blow, the guy will be expecting a knight in full regalia and all he'll see is a boy on a bike."

Jason drew himself up. "Yeah, well this boy and this bike are not just your everyday slobs, you know. I'm going to ride circles around the guy."

William shrugged. Sir Simon hadn't given him anything to do. And what could he do anyway? A tumbling exhibition? With all the fools gathering, there were enough tumblers in the courtyard to hold a meet. No, it was the same old story. Jason was the train jumper and the bicycle knight and he, William, wasn't anything. Fine. So if Jason wanted to be the big hero, let him go ahead and try.

With the next trumpet call, Sir Simon rose to his feet to announce the last event of the morning. "A joust between my good friend, Sir Morlan, of the neighboring kingdom of Haggleshire, and our new friend and esteemed visitor from across the border, the noble Sir Jason of Yorkshire. Gentlemen, to the lists."

"That's you," William said.

Jason flipped down his visor with a decisive clank, mounted his bicycle, and stood at the ready, the unwieldy lance balanced in the crook of his elbow. Sir Simon had instructed him to stay out of sight until the last moment.

In full jousting armor, Sir Morlan entered the courtyard. His big black stallion pranced and danced his way across the drawbridge, fighting his master's tight hold on the reins with defiant tosses of his head. Each drop of his thick hoof echoed against the wooden planks like the warning beat of a drum.

"He sure is big," Jason said as he watched the man circle the courtyard once and take up his place at the far end.

"Which one? The man or the horse?" William asked.

"Both," said Jason in a low voice.

"Bring on your mysterious knight," Sir Morlan roared at his host. Sir Simon stood up and nodded at William who jabbed Jason with his elbow. "Go for it," he said, and Jason wobbled out of his hiding place.

Jason lurched around the edge of the courtyard with his visor bobbing up and down on his head, trying to balance the lance and steer the bike over the bumpy cobblestones at the same time.

Sir Morlan flipped up his own visor in order to see his opponent better. "What is this?" he roared in disbelief. "Sir Simon, you have made a fool of me. You have sent me into the lists against a mere boy and a bumbling one at that. He cannot even afford a horse but must ride about on the wheels of a cart.''

The crowd burst into howls of laughter at the sight of Jason. They pointed and slapped their knees and guffawed. Sir Simon leaned against a friendly baron and wiped the tears of laughter from his eyes. Tolliver came up next to William.

"What do you think of it?'' he asked.

"It's mean and nasty,'' William said. "Everyone is making fun of Jason. And Sir Simon's letting them do it. I'm going to tell him to stop it.''

Tolliver grabbed his arm. "Wait. See what Jason does.''

Jason hadn't given up. He took his appointed position at the opposite end of the courtyard from Sir Morlan. Then he flipped up his visor. "Honorable Knight,'' he shouted. "Are you ready to tilt against me or shall I declare victory by default?''

"Go, Jason,'' William shouted, and from somewhere in the crowd, he heard Gudrin's voice echo the name. The name Jason spread from one person's lips to another until the air fairly buzzed with it. The buzzing escalated to a chant. "JA-SON! JA-SON!'' Sir Simon rose and lifted his hands for silence.

"Let the joust begin. And may the best man win.''

"Man!'' thundered Sir Morlan. "There is only one man here.'' Without further warning, he gave his horse a vicious kick and rode toward Jason, his lance at the ready. As the black stallion galloped the length of the courtyard, Jason once again struggled to get the bike moving on the uneven surface. He'd wobble along for a few feet, drop his foot from the pedal, push off again, and all this while the horse was bearing down on him. The crowd had gone completely silent.

"Move, Jason," William whispered to himself. "For God's sake, move." At the last moment, Jason ducked the parry of the lance and wobbled away in the opposite direction.

But Sir Morlan had pushed his horse to such a head-long gallop that he had to ride across the drawbridge and down a grassy slope to get the stallion turned around again. This gave Jason the time he needed to build up to cruising speed.

"Don't stop again," William cried as Jason drew near on his second turn. "No matter what you do, keep pedaling."

"I know," Jason called as he swept past, his body hunched low over the handlebars. Now the lance was the problem. He couldn't seem to get it balanced right, so half the time the back part of it was dragging on the ground. He ducked two more feints by Sir Morlan, who roared with fury every time the bicycle circled him.

"Stand your ground, boy," he cried. "I cannot see where the devil you are."

"Precisely my plan, Sir Morlan," Jason shouted back as he leaned into a corner.

The crowd clapped and rooted for Jason, who looked more like an irritating horsefly next to the snorting stallion than any kind of real challenger in the lists. Sir Morlan couldn't keep his eye on Jason long enough to unseat him, and Jason's stabs with the lance kept missing.

Deegan appeared. "Looks as if this will go on all day," he said with a smile. "Jason Stubbs Hardy has lived up to his name. He is both stubborn and hearty."

William groaned. "But will it ever end? All Sir Morlan has to do is dig his heels into that horse. Jason's been pedaling for ages and he's looking pretty tired to me."

"Well, then, shall we even things up a bit, Muggins?" asked Deegan with a mischievous lift of his right eyebrow. "A little funning, a little confusion, some distraction for the eye?"

"What eye?"

"Why the eye of the horse, of course. Come along, my good fellow. Follow me," Deegan cried, and catapulted himself into the courtyard with a series of increasingly tight handsprings. So swiftly did he rotate that he was soon nothing but a green blur streaking across the space.

William watched as the fool completed his first circle around the courtyard. It was crazy to do a tumbling pass on the hard cobblestones, but as Deegan headed back in his direction, William's body tensed. He wanted to join the fool.

"He's coming back," Tolliver cried.

When Deegan whirled past for a second turn, William cartwheeled into line behind him. The crowd roared at the sight of them, but William focused only on Deegan as if he could suck from him everything he needed—the energy, the timing, the courage to tumble on uneven cobblestones strewn with straw. It was a crazy and daring display but Deegan gave it his all and by the time they made their second circle together, William had found his old rhythm.

Deegan's idea seemed to be working. With a look of wild alarm, the horse turned this way and that, trying to keep all his attackers in view at once.

Sir Morlan cursed the poor stallion and tried to hold him in one direction while, at the same time, swiveling around in the seat to locate the boy. The horse's momentary confusion gave Jason the split second of advantage he needed, and he charged from the right flank, his lance balanced correctly in his arm for the first and only time. But he misjudged once again, and the lance got stuck in the space between the knight's leg and his saddle.

This was the final blow for the poor horse. He took off at a dead run for the drawbridge, with Sir Morlan roaring at him to stop and Jason hanging on for dear life.

"LET GO, JASON!" William screamed as he came up from his last dizzying cartwheel. "LET GO OF THE LANCE!" But by that time, Jason seemed to be frozen in his peculiar position. The last they saw of him, he was headed across the moat, one hand steering the handlebars and the other clamped to the hilt of his weapon the way a drowning man clings to a piece of driftwood.

Up on the ramparts, the crowd rushed to the other side of the wall walk and called down reports. "They're over the moat, down the hill, now." "We've lost them. They've galloped out of sight."

A stillness settled over the courtyard. Everybody turned toward Sir Simon, who rose to his feet and looked around in a bewildered way.

Without any warning, Deegan came up behind William, picked him up with one easy lift and settled him onto his shoulders. William was too surprised to object. One minute he was on the ground, his mind in a blur, and the next, he was sitting high up like a boy at a holiday parade. They walked toward the drawbridge.

"Deegan," Sir Simon shouted. "What are you doing?"

"Going to welcome home the hero," Deegan called back without turning around.

"I wish you weren't leaving," William said to the air.

"A fool cannot do the same tricks he did yesterday, my good William. And I have tricks for trade. You teach me yours, I'll teach you mine."

"But what happens if—"

"If what?"

"If the ship comes back?"

"I am nothing but a fool, boy."

"Will you know if we need you? Will you come then?"

"I come, I go. Half past yesterday, twenty minutes to tomorrow. I am the man of the moment, reinventing myself every day. I have told you before. A fool is not to be counted on."

"Lucky you," William muttered to himself from his perch.

"So, half-man, half-boy, what do you see?" Deegan said when he stopped in the center of the drawbridge.

"Someone's coming back," came a shout from the top of the wall walk.

"Which one?" called a chorus of voices.

"It's Jason," said William in a hushed voice. "Jason's the one coming back."

"Sir Jason of Yorkshire returns," Deegan announced in ringing tones, and once more the ramparts

sang with the chant of his name. "JA-SON, JA-SON."
William slid from Deegan's shoulders.

Deegan put a hand out and caught him by the arm.
"You will not see me again for some time, half-boy,
half-man," he whispered with a strange kind of ur-
gency. "And you will be angry with me."

"Why?" William asked impatiently.

The fool shrugged and grinned at the same time, but
he didn't answer. His face took on the expression of an
irresponsible little boy and William didn't like it. He
pulled roughly away and ran down the hill to meet his
friend.

"Are you all right?" he asked.

Jason nodded wearily. William took the bike from
him.

"You can take the helmet off now," he said, and
Jason lifted it from his head. His glasses hung askew
and one lens was cracked down the middle. Little drops
of sweat ran down his temples but he didn't seem to
notice.

"Good you did all that training."

Jason managed a grin. "Best workout I've had in
weeks."

"What happened to Sir Morlan?"

"You saw how the lance got caught between his leg
and the saddle. Down at the bottom of the hill, he
shifted his weight enough so the lance fell out."

"Then what?"

"He shouted at me that Sir Simon should meet him at the border. He was tired of playing games with a boy. Then he rode off."

"Some boy," said William, and he gave his friend a punch on the shoulder.

"Ouch," said Jason. "That hurts. Everything hurts."

From opposite corners of the wall walk, the trumpets rang out. With the creak of leather and the staccato rattle of hoofbeats against wood, the great procession was finally under way. Sir Simon, on Moonlight, was leading the entourage. When the group reached the two boys, Sir Simon put up his hand for silence.

"My noble friend, you have done well. In all my years in the lists, never have I seen such a joust."

Jason bowed.

"Young William, our good friend and yours, defends himself with his body as he has already proved. But you are a squire in need of a weapon." Sir Simon drew from his sheath a long thin sword with a golden hilt. "Sir Jason of Yorkshire, I leave you this. Use it wisely in defense of my kingdom until my return."

Jason took the sword. He extended his arms and lifted the weapon for all to see. The sword glittered in the sun as he turned in a slow triumphant semicircle.

The people went wild with excitement. They chanted his name and stamped their feet at the sight of their new hero.

William stood aside to let Sir Simon pass. With a final wave, the knight loosed the reins on Moonlight and the impatient horse broke into a full canter. Soon the whole procession was thundering down the path between William and Jason. The dust rose with the incessant thrumming of their hoofbeats. The horseflesh and the brightly colored drapes and the flash of silver armor in the sun all blurred into one long noisy wall of sound and color that seemed to go on forever.

CHAPTER 10

Life in the castle slowly returned to normal. Jason went to bed the afternoon that Sir Simon left and slept straight through until the next morning. The extra retainers hired for the feast wrapped up their meager belongings and took themselves home. The blacksmith and the cobbler packed their tools and trundled back down the castle path to their villages. For an entire day, a steady stream of people poured across the drawbridge, and the guard in the gatehouse did not bother to drop the portcullis except at night.

The instant Jason woke up, Tolliver began begging him for lessons on the bicycle.

"Is it all right if he uses yours?" Jason asked.

"Sure, it's fine," said William. He left them together, with Jason starting in on his endurance lecture.

William found Gudrin down in the kitchen, preparing a tray for her uncle. They hadn't spoken since they first arrived at the castle and now William felt awkward around her. He wondered if she'd seen his tumbling exhibition.

"The place seems pretty quiet all of a sudden," he said. "Did you see Deegan leave?"

She shook her head. "Nobody ever sees Deegan leave. One minute he's here, the next he's gone."

"I wish he were still here," William said. "What if the ship comes back or some enemy attacks from the border or Calendar's evil thing appears?"

"But what would Deegan do?" Gudrin asked. "He's nothing but a fool."

William had heard that line too many times before. "How's your uncle?" he asked.

"Quite cheery this morning, actually," she said. "He's been doing exercises. Says he wishes to be prepared to defend Sir Simon's castle and his honor." She picked up the tray. "He wants to see you."

Dick lived in a room at the very top of the inner gatehouse. When they arrived, he was trotting around the outer edges of the small circular space. A black cat was sitting under a table in the center of the room. He paid no attention to the man but concentrated instead on washing his paws.

"That's Calendar's cat," William said. "The one who was the dragon."

"Yes. He keeps me company," Dick said. "The poor thing thinks I've gone quite mad this morning."

"Well, you do seem to have regained some of your old spirit, sir," said William. He hunkered down next to the cat and they stared at each other for a moment. "Same eyes," William said at last. "I remember them from when I faced him as the dragon."

"He's getting old now but he's still a good ratter. He keeps the castle free of the vermin," Dick said as he sat down to his breakfast. "Will you join me?"

"I've already eaten," William said. "But I'll sit with you."

Gudrin had settled herself on the stone bench near the window. Her head was bent over a piece of embroidery but William felt her eyes on him.

"I find I have quite an appetite this morning," Dick said. " 'Tis good to get the blood moving a bit, I expect. I told Gudrin I wished to speak to you."

"Yes," William said.

"Although we have nothing to fear, we must be prepared at all times. I have spoken to the guards, but you and Jason and I should check on them regularly to be sure they have secured the watch. They have a tendency to slacken off when Sir Simon's away."

"Yes, sir." William glanced at Gudrin, who flashed

an unexpected smile at him. Her uncle's good mood must have lifted her own. Dick went on about checking the armory and keeping the horses exercised and William kept nodding and agreeing, all the while wondering how he could get Gudrin to hang out with him for the day.

"About the horses, sir," he said suddenly.

"Yes?"

"Gudrin and I could exercise two of them. She could give me some riding instruction at the same time. That would be useful, I think."

"Splendid idea, my boy," Dick said, clapping him on the back.

"I have some work to finish here, Uncle," Gudrin said.

"She always has work to do. Out roaming in the fields like a wild thing and then studying over those books night and day. I should never have allowed Deegan to teach you to read, my girl," Dick said.

Gudrin did not lift her head.

"You will meet young William in the stables this afternoon, won't you?"

"If you insist, Uncle."

"After the noon meal?" William asked.

"Suit yourself," she said with a shrug. But she did not sound totally disappointed.

*　　*　　*

They made a deal. She would teach him how to ride a horse, and in the evenings when nobody was watching, he would teach her how to ride his bike. The first afternoon, she made him saddle her horse as well as his. She was a tough taskmaster.

"Poke him in the belly before you cinch up," she said. "Sorrel likes to fill up with air, and before you know it, the saddle's slipped and you're hanging upside down."

They rode down the castle path, and as soon as they were over the crest of the first hill, she dismounted, tied up her thick skirts, and swung her leg over the saddle.

"Alan, that red-faced guard on watch today, is a terrible tattletale. He tells my uncle when I do something unseemly. It is unseemly for a girl to straddle a horse," she scoffed. "No use upsetting Uncle Dick any more."

"He seems different this morning."

"Perhaps he has been too long under Sir Simon's thumb," she said. "I think he's happy to be in charge of the castle. You know, a lot of map snapping and plan making and busy preparations." She grinned as she whipped Sorrel into a full gallop. "Come on now," she called back over her shoulder. "No time for idle chatter."

Without any warning, William's horse, a chestnut mare named Mandrake, followed suit. William grabbed the mane and hung on for dear life until Gudrin reined in and shouted instructions to him from alongside. "Squeeze your knees. Lean forward. Tighten up on your reins."

She was just as hard on herself. Every evening after supper, William took her out to a clearing behind the castle to practice on the bike. She didn't seem to have any natural sense of balance, and with her unwieldy skirts constantly coming undone and getting tangled in the pedals, ten wobbly yards were her limit. But she stuck with it. William was the one who called off the sessions because of darkness.

Jason knew that William was learning how to ride a horse but he didn't seem jealous. He was too involved in setting up Tolliver's training schedule and teaching him basic bike maintenance. Tolliver loved the attention.

"I've been timing him with the stopwatch," Jason said one night when he and William were lying on their pallets in the darkness. "He's pretty good for a little kid. We should take him back with us and enter him in a few races."

"No way."

"Just kidding. But he seems to love the sport as much as I do."

"Or else he's just stubborn," William said. "Like his cousin."

"Why does she keep her bike riding such a secret?"

"She says she has to or Dick will put a stop to it. Girls aren't allowed to do anything in this day and age. She doesn't even know how to swim. And she's probably the only girl in the whole kingdom who knows how to read and write."

William and Gudrin fell into an easy way of being together. He cheered the first time she careened around the castle on the bike without taking her feet from the pedals. In the mornings, they took longer and longer rides. He brought along his binoculars and showed her how to use them and she pointed out the birds to him and named them.

"How do you know their names?" he asked.

"My grandmother taught me," she said.

"Did she tell you to pick all those plants too?"

"Yes," said Gudrin. "She taught me about herbs and their healing powers. I have already cured a young boy of his toothache and two women of boils on their backs. I know how to make poultices, and that bitter root cures dropsy and scrofulous disorders and—"

"Enough," said William, putting up his hands. "I believe you."

"Most boys aren't interested," she said with a note of contempt in her voice.

"Listen, my mother's a doctor too," he said. "I hear about this stuff all the time."

*   *   *

"You've found your seat," she said one morning as they pulled up to open a gate. She was looking into the distance the way she did when she said something nice.

"What does that mean?"

"You and the horse move as if you are one."

"Yes," he said. "That's just the way it feels."

"Does it ever happen with the bicycle?"

William leaned over to undo the gate and backed Mandrake away to let her through. "You'll have to ask Jason that. It never happened to me with the bicycle. Only with gymnastics."

"Gymnastics?"

"Tumbling, I mean."

"Oh yes. I remember. I saw you following Deegan around the courtyard."

Did she think he was good? he wondered, but he didn't dare ask. He kicked the gate closed with his foot and she fastened it. "Come on," she called as she dug her heels into Sorrel. "Today we'll go all the way to the harbor and back."

It was a wild and wonderful ride. The sun lay warm on William's shoulders and the wind streamed through his hair and the sea of blue cornflowers stretched away as far as the eye could see. He urged Mandrake up next to Sorrel, and the two horses matched stride. Gudrin glanced over at him, then threw her head back and laughed wildly in a way he had never seen her do before. For the first time, she looked carefree and playful but also a little crazy, and he was reminded of Calendar and the look in her eye the day she turned Alastor to lead. He was scared suddenly at how far he had come from home. He felt as if he were riding away from everything that he knew before, from everything that was familiar. His parents and the attic and school and gymnastics, they all felt like some hazy dream that he had dreamed in another life and that he might never be able to dream again.

Gudrin reined in above the small curve in the shoreline that she called the harbor. They slid off their horses and led them down to the little strip of beach where the fishermen pulled up their dories to sort the day's catch.

All the boats had put to sea except for one. An old man sat on its gunwale mending his nets.

"Good day to you, sir," said Gudrin.

"And to you, miss," he said without looking up. There was a surly tone to his voice. "If the day is good to you, then you would do well to move away from this place."

"The day is not good for you, sir?" William asked.

"Lady Luck has turned against me. My nets rip, the

boat leaks. It's been that way for some days now. Ever since that death ship floated in on the tide.''

Gudrin and William looked at each other.

"But that was some time ago," William said quickly. "Sir Simon had it towed away."

"Yes, well, my good boy, he did not tow it far enough. It's come back. Two nights ago. On the high tide.''

William scanned the horizon.

"It's down east a league or two and it's getting closer every day. The tide that brought it in will not take it out again. And the ship is not beached. It floats in the deepest water close into shore. Just around there," he muttered with a nod over his shoulder. "It's from the headlands you see it. Ever since the nasty thing came back, the nets come up empty. We are fishing much farther out to sea than we usually do but it does no good. And some of the men never come back at all. I do believe the very ocean has been poisoned.''

Gudrin led William back the way they had come and then took a left through a thick stand of gorse bushes. From there they followed the steep rocky path that climbed the headlands.

"You brought the binoculars?" Gudrin called over her shoulder as she reached the top of the rise.

He patted his belt pack.

"Better get them out," she said, pointing straight down. "There it is. In the lee of the shore."

At first glance, the ship looked like any other. It was a one-masted vessel with what had once been a square sail and high turreted edges at the bow and stern.

But this ship had an unnatural look about it. The breeze and the current seemed to have no effect on it at all. The sail hung in long dirty strips like hair ribbons, and the rudder flapped idly back and forth on its own irregular schedule. The sea did not lift this vessel or shift its position in any way.

"Give me the binoculars," Gudrin said, and he handed them to her without even looking through them first. He wasn't sure he wanted to see what was down there.

Gudrin sat still for such a long time that Sorrel put his head down for a snack. He curled his long lips around some tufts of brown grass and ripped them from their roots. Mandrake snorted and blew, searching for thistles. Only Gudrin's head moved as she slowly scanned the decks of the ship from bow to stern and back again.

Finally William couldn't stand it anymore. "What is it? What do you see?"

"Bones," she said without lowering the glasses. "Some connected, some just scattered around. And odd bits of clothing and debris."

''There were bones and garbage in the river that day. Are you sure?''

''The skeleton ship. See for yourself,'' she muttered and handed over the binoculars. ''Come to ravage / Come to kill / Bones will crack / Blood will spill.'' At the lilting chant of her voice, Mandrake stirred uneasily and briefly lifted her head to look at the girl.

The binoculars were lightweight, small enough to fit in William's belt pack, so the magnification wasn't particularly strong. But he could see enough. Sometimes the bones of the sailor were laid out in perfect formation as if the man had fallen in his tracks and his flesh and organs had been sucked away in one single instant, leaving the skeleton undisturbed. But in other places on the deck, William could see a skull here, a foot there, as if whatever had stripped the meat away had tossed the bones aside like so many pieces of trash.

He yanked the binoculars from his eyes. For a minute he thought that he might be sick, but he had never thrown up and he wasn't going to do it now in front of a girl. He forced himself to breathe deeply, to the diaphragm, as Coach would say, once, twice, another time. The feeling of nausea passed and he busied himself with putting the binoculars away. Mandrake was up to her neck in a gorse bush, and with a gentle kick and a tug on the reins, he backed her out. Still Gudrin said nothing. She sat on Sorrel and stared down at that ship as if she had nowhere else to go, nothing else to think about, as if by sheer force of will she could make the ship disappear.

When she turned toward him, she was changed. There was a wild look in her eyes that shocked him. It was as if some animal were peering out at him through her face.

"We have to burn it," she said. "We have to come back tonight and burn it."

"Let's go tell your uncle about it," William suggested. "He'll know what to do."

"He'll do nothing," muttered Gudrin. "He wouldn't listen to my grandmother. That's why he let them lock her up in that convent. He won't listen to you or me either. If we show him the ship, he'll just wring his hands and worry. Or have it towed out to sea again. And it will return. I know that now. We have to destroy it."

She yanked Sorrel's head out of the grass and wheeled the horse around. William reined Mandrake in and let her gallop ahead of them down the path. It was no use killing themselves getting back to the castle, he thought, as he let his horse take her time going down.

They rode most of the way in silence. When the castle loomed into view, she looked at William.

"Are you with me?" she asked.

When he didn't answer right away, she pulled Sorrel

to a stop in the middle of the path. William trotted on
for a short distance and then circled back to her.

"It doesn't matter to me," she said. "If I have to,
I'll do it alone."

"We're just kids, you know. We shouldn't have to
do things like this," he said, but as soon as the words
were out of his mouth, he wished he could take them
back. They sounded pathetic.

"I'm with you," he said at last.

"What about Jason?" she asked.

"What about him?"

"Can we trust him to help us?"

"First you're saying you can do this alone and you
don't need us!" he exploded. "Now you want a torch-
ing party."

She stared at him calmly like a teacher waiting for
the answer to a question.

"Of course we can trust him. He'd love it." William
threw up his hands. "Burning boats at midnight. One
of his favorite occupations."

"Good. Tell him to bring the bicycle. We'll need
his panniers to carry the torches and he can be an extra
pair of hands in the dory."

William watched as she urged Sorrel into a canter.
He should have refused, he thought. He should have
let her just try and burn up that boat by herself. She'd
see.

CHAPTER 11

In the dead-still night, every noise seemed magnified to William. The loading of the long wooden torches into a fisherman's dory, Gudrin's whispered instructions to the boys to push it into the water, the scrape of the oars against the oarlocks. William pulled on one oar and Jason on the other while Gudrin sat in the bow directing them. They had given her the flashlight from William's backpack, and for a while, she played with the strange object, flicking the switch on and off and making light circles in the inky sky above them. Finally she settled down and concentrated on getting them in striking distance of the ship.

William had to keep lifting his oar and waiting for Jason to catch up. Jason had great biking muscles in his legs but William had more strength in his arms from all those years of floor exercises.

"We almost there?" Jason called to Gudrin.

She didn't bother to answer.

"Shh," William said for about the tenth time.

"Why do we have to be so quiet?" Jason whispered back. "After all, there's nothing out here but a pile of bones."

"You didn't see them," William said with a shiver. "Even from a distance, they looked pretty creepy."

"Well, they're not going to jump off that ship and grab us, are they?" Jason said. "You can't hear us anymore can you, old boys?" he called out, cupping his hand around his mouth. I bet he's just as scared as I am, William thought. Jason always shows off when he's nervous.

"We're pulling to the right again," Gudrin called softly from the bow. "Straighten out, the ship's in sight."

William let his oar rest on the surface of the water to give Jason time to swing them around. He cocked his head and listened and knew suddenly what was missing. When he was eight, his parents had taken him sailing for three days. At night, when he lay in his bunk, he heard the slap of the halyard against the mast, the splash of the waves along the hull, and the creak of metal rings rubbing one another. The fittings of this ghostly ship made no sound because the sea and the wind had no hold on it. The currents did not move it, the breeze did not lift the shredded sails, the waves did not rock it back and forth. They might as well have been rowing toward a black hole in the ocean for all the noise it made.

"We'll head up above the ship and let the current take us down toward it," Gudrin said. "Then the wind will be at our backs when we throw the torches. Start pulling again, William. And please try to keep it even this time."

"Pushy lady," Jason whispered under his breath. "What I don't understand is this. We're breaking our backs rowing against the current to get to this stupid ship. Why isn't it floating toward us?"

So Jason had noticed it too. William shrugged. He didn't want to waste his breath trying to explain. He was using all of it to row.

They eased their way around the stern and swung upward into the wind which had picked up in the last few minutes.

"Keep going, row away from it a little more," Gudrin said. She had to lift her voice above the sudden breeze. "We need some extra time to get the torches ready."

They did as she ordered, happy to put some distance between themselves and the heavy dark shadow of the ship. They held the dory into the wind while Gudrin pulled out the long wooden torches and lined them up against the gunwales. Then when she signaled that she was ready, they shipped their oars, and the three of them leaned together to make a shelter against the wind so the matches could catch. Good thing I brought these, William thought, but he didn't say anything. As the oil-soaked rags caught fire, Gudrin handed them out. By the time the dory drifted back down with the current, each of them held two burning torches.

In the sudden dancing light, William glanced at Gudrin. Her skin shone and her hair floated in a wild tangle above her head. Her eyes were fixed on the ship, and in a sudden graceful movement, she rose to her feet and hurled the first torch with her left hand and then the second with her right. The first hit the edge of the forecastle and plummeted into the sea with a sizzle. The second arched high into the sky and landed squarely in the middle of the deck.

"Throw yours," she cried, her voice suddenly frantic. "Go on, hurry."

Jason looked at William. "We've got to stand together," he said. "Otherwise the boat will capsize. Sit down, Gudrin," he called, and she melted into her seat without a word.

"One, two, three," William said, as they stood and tossed in unison, with their right hands and then their left. Jason's first torch sailed over the ship and landed in the sea on the other side, but the other three torches hit the deck. The trail of flames lit up the night sky like a Fourth of July celebration.

Water was slopping over the gunwales of the dory

but Gudrin didn't seem to notice. Up in the bow, she was fiddling with the matches, trying to light another three torches. "Help me with these stupid things!" she screamed at William, shaking the matchbox.

He glanced at her and then over the bow again. The wind had carried them down to within a few feet of the death ship. They were going to ram it.

William pulled Jason down into the boat. "Start rowing again, fast!" William yelled. "We're too close to throw anything."

He and Jason bent over the oars, and just before their own little boat crashed into the massive dark hull, they managed to ease the bow around so that it cut through the swells. Slowly they began to make some headway, but with the rise and fall of each wave, Gudrin was getting drenched. She didn't pay any attention.

"Look," she cried, pointing up at the deck of the boat. "They're not catching. We've got to light more."

"Watch the box of matches," Jason shouted at her. "Keep them dry if you can. And the torches too."

Crouched over his oar, William wondered if the two of them had gone mad. He didn't care anymore about burning the ship, he just wanted to get as far away from it as possible. When they had first come out here, the sea had been calm as a pond on a hot summer afternoon. Now it felt angry, stirred up, dangerous.

"We're getting too far from shore," he yelled in Jason's ear. "Let's turn. The current will take us around the bow, and we can toss the torches from there."

Jason nodded and lifted his oar. The dory spun as if caught in a whirlpool, and William was hit full in the face with the next wave. Gudrin leapt to her feet and screamed against the noise of the wind, "It caught, it caught."

"Sit down," Jason yelled, and he reached behind and tugged at her thick burlap skirt. The dory was going over. William scrambled to the stern to try and right the boat, but he was too late. Everything seemed to happen in slow motion. As he slid into the water, William looked up one more time. Gudrin was right, he thought. The last thing he saw before the waves closed over his head were long skinny flames dancing up the mast and licking the sails.

The water was bone-chilling, the kind of cold that makes your chest tighten and close up. With clumsy, sodden strokes, William fought his way to the surface. When he broke through and took in those first precious gulps of air, the sky was lit up so brightly that for a moment he thought he had spent the night underwater and a new day had dawned. But of course it was the fire. The flames shot up into the sky, and as he watched, the top of the mast tipped slowly sideways and plummeted into the sea like a flaming rocket.

"We did it, Gudrin," he cried. "You were right. We did it."

Gudrin. Where was she? She couldn't swim. And with those heavy skirts . . .

"Gudrin!" he screamed again. He shoved aside the debris from the dory that was floating upside down near him and paddled madly in one direction.

"JASON," he cried. "Where are you? Where's Gudrin?"

From the other side of the dory, William heard an answering call.

"I'm here," Jason cried. "But I can't find her."

William swam up to the bow where she had been sitting, and began to dive down, over and over again, his hands reaching out in the cold murky water for any sign of her. Please, let us find her, please, don't let her die, please, please, please. Up he came for another gulp of air and then down again. Just when he knew he didn't have enough strength for one more dive, his left hand touched something, a sodden mass of rough clothing. He grabbed and pulled the whole weight of it upward, fighting the pressure of the water against him. He burst through the surface, filled his aching lungs with air, and with a last spurt of energy, he dragged her body up onto the edge of the dory. Behind him the fire raged on, and he was stunned by the roaring noise it made. The orange flames lit up Gudrin's face. Her eyes were closed and she wasn't breathing.

"Jason, I found her," he called. "Over on this side."

Every time he let go of Gudrin's waist to pound her between the shoulder blades, her body began to slide down the steep hull of the dory, back into the sea. Then, suddenly, he got mad. She had gotten them into this mess. He was not going to let her go and die on them.

"Breathe, Gudrin, blast you," he yelled. "Your stupid ship is burning. Wake up and watch it." He pounded her once more on the back. This time the slap was so hard that her head shook.

"Hey, old buddy, go easy," Jason said from Gudrin's other side. "You're going to kill her."

William didn't answer because Gudrin's mouth had opened and a torrent of water was pouring out of it. She choked and coughed and spat, and another bucketful spewed forth. At last her eyes opened and she stared at William without moving. She looked like a baby taking a nap, with the slimy planking of the dory as her pillow.

"Are you all right?" William called.

A wave splashed over her face.

"Help me hold on to her," he yelled at Jason.

Jason grabbed her around the waist. It took all their strength to keep her from sliding underwater again. She stared blankly at William.

"I think she's in some kind of shock," William said. "Start kicking toward shore. As long as we hold on to the dory, we should be all right."

Jason nodded, and wearily they began to move their legs back and forth. The current had carried them slightly downwind of the ship, but they were close enough to feel the heat of the fire. The pitch that had been used to caulk the hull was burning, and a noxious black smoke billowed up above the flames and floated over their heads.

Suddenly William heard strange plops in the water all around them.

"What's that?" Jason called. "What's falling out of the sky?"

William twisted and turned, and in among the chunks of charred wood and barrels and old ropes, he saw small moving bodies, black shapes, paddling for shore alongside them. More and more were raining down around them all the time.

"Rats," he mouthed as one of the creatures scrambled up on the hull of the dory. It soon lost its footing on the wet surface and began sliding toward Gudrin's motionless head. William let go of her so he could sweep it away with his hand. The sleek oily body disappeared for a moment under the water and then surfaced again, just to the left of them.

"Kick," Jason screamed. "Splash. Make noise. Anything to keep them away."

The thought of the creatures brushing past them gave the boys new life and energy. Gudrin lifted her head briefly and then sank into her previous position, her glazed eyes resting on William. Her look chilled him. It seemed as if she had given all her power over to him, as if she no longer cared what happened to her now that she had put him in charge.

"Come on, Gudrin, kick some," he said in her ear. "We're closer to shore now."

And again, like a robot under his command, she began to move her feet in weak, ineffectual circles.

"The rats don't really care about us," Jason called to him. "See, they just want to make it to shore as fast as we do."

William didn't have the strength to answer.

Behind them the skeleton ship continued to burn, and every so often with an exploding pop, some spar or rudder section would split off and drop like a bomb into the sea.

Just when William thought his arm would break from holding on to Gudrin and his feet would never be able to feel anything again, they touched bottom. The boys pushed the boat in as far as it would go and slid

Gudrin off the side of the hull. Her legs crumpled under her. They half dragged, half carried her up the narrow strip of beach. The three of them collapsed into a shivering wet heap.

"We can't just lie here," Jason said between chattering teeth. "Either we'll freeze to death or the rats will bite us."

All around them the rats squeaked as they gained the shore and scuttled about on the sand.

"Rub your arms," William said as he struggled to a sitting position. "Flap them around. We've got to get the circulation moving. Come on, Gudrin, wake up. You'll catch pneumonia lying there."

Again she did as she was told, and it wasn't long before the three of them were slapping each other on the back and pounding their heels into the sand. Then William and Jason dragged Gudrin to her feet, and they danced around and around in a circle like three whirling maniacs.

"Look," Jason cried, pulling them to a stop. He pointed down the beach. Lined up like battalions, the rats stood and waited in neatly formed rows, facing out to sea.

"What are they looking at?" Gudrin asked.

Nobody answered. All eyes had shifted to the ship. Silhouetted against the dying flames, a tall black figure stood on the gunwales.

"What in God's name is that?" Jason whispered.

"It's a rat," said William. "A huge rat. Standing on its back legs like a person does."

Gudrin stood between them. "William," she said without taking her eyes off the ship. "It's the one Calendar warned us about. Remember the chant? Evil lurking, evil rising / Washed in with the tide."

"It's just a bunch of rats," Jason said, but his voice wavered.

"Let's go," said William.

"Look," Gudrin said, and she pointed at the ship.

The biggest rat raised its front legs to the sky, and just before the flames engulfed it, it threw itself into the black sea.

The rats on the beach held their ranks, but a tumult of excited squeaking ran along the line as they followed the progress of the last lone figure paddling smoothly toward shore.

"Never satisfied / Till we all have died," Gudrin finished in her low chanting voice.

William wasn't going to wait to see more. He grabbed Gudrin by the hand and started sprinting for the path with Jason close behind. Up at the top, he boosted her onto her horse.

"Can you ride?" he asked.

She nodded, and he could see her eyes, once again, wide and frightened and questioning. He looked away.

He didn't have any answers for her. By burning the ship, it seemed they had let something far worse than skeletons loose in the world. They had to get back to the castle as fast as they could ride. Then they could pull up the drawbridge and drop the portcullis and pray that a six-foot rat and its followers would just float on by.

CHAPTER 12

Gudrin was gone in the morning.

"Where?" William asked.

Jason shrugged. "I don't know. She left you a note," he said, handing it over. "It must be very private because it's sealed with wax."

William groaned as he settled himself on a bench outside the buttery. "I feel as if a horse walked over my back," he said.

"Probably from all that swimming," Jason said. "Uses different muscles."

Don't let Jason start in on muscles, William thought as he ripped through the blue wax. He scanned the letter quickly and then reread it, trying to make sense of it. Deegan had better come back soon and work on Gudrin's spelling, he thought with a grin. It felt good to smile at anything.

"Gun to cunvent on Sorel. To sea Sister. Wate for me."

"Where does she think I'm going?" William muttered to himself. He handed the letter to Jason.

"Who's Sister?" Jason asked.

"Must be one of the nuns. We'd better have a little talk with Dick. Tell him what we saw last night."

"He'll never believe us," Jason said. "Not in a million years."

"Even so we should try to convince him."

Their eyes met. "Maybe they went the other way," Jason said. "Along the headlands."

"Maybe," William said.

They found Dick down in the courtyard running around and around the outer edges in wider and wider circles. They waved at him to stop. His face was bright red.

"You'd better slow down," Jason said. "You've got to work up to these things slowly."

"No time like the present, my boy," Dick said, throwing a few punches into the air for good measure. "Now speak your piece, my friends. As you can see, I'm a busy man."

William started. While Dick listened, he continued to jog in place and twist his shoulders back and forth as if preparing for a boxing match.

"It sounds as if you had quite an adventure last

night," he said at last. "Naturally, I do not approve of your dragging my niece off on wild midnight rides."

"Who dragged who?" Jason muttered, but Dick went right on. "I have not seen Gudrin this morning. It is not like her to stay in bed this late."

"She's gone to the convent to see Sister," William said. "Who's Sister?"

"I expect she means Sister Beatrice. She took care of my wife's mother at the end."

"So she must have heard the prophecy," William said. "About the evil that was coming."

"A lot of nonsense," Dick said with a frown. "Dear Calendar was not well in her last days."

"Dick, listen to us," William said. "Here it is once again, pure and simple. The skeleton ship came back last night, and we burned it. And thousands of rats swarmed off the ship." He shuddered at the memory. "And they may be headed this way."

"Well, no matter," said Dick. "I told you Calendar's cat is one of the best ratters around. And besides that, we have stray cats in the stable. They keep us awake at night with their howling and carrying on. Perhaps now they'll be of some use to us."

"Dick, this isn't just one or two rats," Jason said. "There's a beachful of them out there. Enough to fill this courtyard."

"And one of them was huge," William said.

"Bigger than the cat?"

Jason and William glanced at each other. "Bigger than you, Dick," William said. "Taller. It stood up on its hind legs."

He looked from one to the other of them with his brow furrowed. "Are you quite sure, boys?"

"Yes," said Jason. "We're positive."

He laid a hand on each of their foreheads. "Calendar always warned me that the sea air at night addled the brain. I do think, boys, you should go back to your pallets and take a little more rest. Perhaps when you wake for the second time, these strange delusions will have passed."

He waved away their objections and returned to his jogging. "Go on, now, be off with you," he called.

"Don't say 'I told you so,' " William warned as they headed to the buttery to scrounge up some breakfast.

"I told you so," Jason said.

They settled down to wait. They pretended not to. Jason got Tolliver back on the bike and trained him as if there were no tomorrow. William exercised Mandrake that day and the next, but he didn't dare travel too far from the castle for fear he would miss something. He spent the rest of his time up on the ramparts with Brian, prowling back and forth along the wall with his binoculars held to his eyes.

"What are you looking for, Sir William?"

"Trouble," was all William said. After talking to Dick, he and Jason had decided they wouldn't try to convince anybody else about the monster rat. "When Miss Gudrin goes out like this, how long does she usually stay?"

"One never knows," Brian replied. "Poor orphaned child. She's a roamer, more at home in the fields than in the castle. She journeyed often to the convent to see her grandmother in the old woman's last days."

"Did you think Calendar was mad?" William asked.

"It's not my place to say, but you know, she never really recovered from that other time. From himself."

"You mean, Alastor," said William.

"I do not choose to speak his name," Brian replied with a shudder. "We shall not see the likes of him again, Sir William."

"I hope not, Brian. For all our sakes." But perhaps there are things in the world even worse than Alastor, William thought. It had occurred to him that if they had never burnt the ship, the rats might have stayed on it forever. But it was no use thinking about that now. They had done what they had done, and now they had to live with the consequences.

He swept the binoculars across the road leading up to the castle from the west and stopped at the sight of a dark shadow rounding the last corner. "Someone's coming," he said. "It's Miss Gudrin. Finally." He handed the glasses over to Brian who put them up to his nose.

"You're looking through them the wrong way," William called as he sprinted for the tower steps. "Switch them around. And give the order to lower the drawbridge. I'll raise the portcullis. Jason," he called down into the courtyard. "Gudrin's back."

She looked tired as she urged Sorrel up the wooden planking of the drawbridge. Her hair was wilder and more unruly than ever, and she clung to the horse's mane with both her hands. Large burlap sacks stuffed with herbs swung from either side of the saddle behind her legs.

William ran to catch Sorrel's halter so Gudrin could slide off before the horse found his own way to the stable and a bucket of oats.

"Did you see any sign of the rats in the countryside?" William asked. He released Sorrel and the horse trotted off.

Gudrin shook her head. "But I was headed in the other direction, away from the coast."

"Why did you go?" Jason asked.

"I wanted to tell Sister Beatrice. She was the only one besides me and Deegan who believed my grandmother's prophecies. And she knows herbal medicine."

"Herbs can't drive away a crowd of rats, Gudrin," William said.

Tolliver was looking from one to the other of them. "Do you really think they're coming this way?" he asked.

"Who told him?" Gudrin asked.

"I did," said Jason. "At least *he* believed me. Your uncle thinks we have addled brains. But my addled brain is just waking up. William, what about the token? We can use the token on them."

"Of course!" William shouted. "Of course!"

"Where is it?" Jason asked.

"The backpack."

"Are you sure?"

"Sure, I'm sure," said William.

"Let's go get it," Jason said.

Gudrin looked puzzled. "What are you two prattling on about? What token?"

"It shrinks things," Tolliver said.

"Take my bike," Jason said as he handed it to Tolliver.

"Wait," Tolliver said. "There's something I have to—"

"Later," Jason called. He and William sprinted across the courtyard toward their bedchamber.

It was gone.

"What do you mean?" said Jason, his voice sounding panicky. "Go through your stuff again." He knelt beside William and began scrambling through the clothes and old potato chip bags. "It's got to be here."

William sat back on his heels. "It's not there, Jason."

"Maybe you hid it somewhere else in the room," Jason said. "Think. Maybe you put it in a pocket of your jeans."

"Deegan took it," said Tolliver's voice from the door. "That's what I was trying to tell you."

"Deegan! Why?" William said, and Jason cried, "How do you know?"

"He showed it to me as he left the castle," Tolliver said. "Made me promise to keep it a secret until he was well away. He's going to use it at the fools' feast. A trick to outdo all the tricksters. He said he'll bring it back when he returns."

"When he returns!" William said. "But that's not for another week, at least. We need it right now."

"I knew there was something shifty about him," Jason said.

Tolliver was scuffing the toe of his soft shoe back and forth along the stone floor. "I'm sorry, Sir William," he said. "I should have told you."

"What good would that have done?" William said. "Deegan seems able to disappear whenever he feels like it. We would never have found him."

Tolliver brightened suddenly. "I could go after him

on the bike,'' he cried. ''Bring them back. After all, Sir Simon's castle is under siege.''

''Not yet, little cousin,'' said Gudrin in a weary voice from behind him. ''And until the castle is attacked, we will have a hard time convincing Uncle that you should go. I've just been to see him. He is furious with all this talk of rats. He says I have gone as batty as our grandmother and if I persist, he will have to lock me up too.''

She looked as if she might cry, and William felt sorry for her. In the last year, she had lost her grandmother and her mother and her aunt. She was only twelve years old, after all. The girls he knew back home were worried about their clothes and their math grades. It seemed unfair that she should have so much on her shoulders. He jumped up.

''Well, we have each other at least,'' he said in as cheery a voice as he could muster. ''We'll keep our eyes open and report anything out of the ordinary to the others. Maybe the rats will pass us by. We have no way of knowing. Gudrin, you must go to sleep now,'' he ordered in a voice that surprised all of them and himself too. ''You're too tired to be of any use like this. The rest of us should go about our business as usual.''

They did as they were told, grateful, it seemed, that somebody was taking charge. Jason and Tolliver went back to their courtyard endurance runs. Every so often, they called up to Brian to let down the drawbridge, and they would circle the castle on their bikes. Jason called it a reconnaissance.

"What does that mean?" Tolliver asked over supper that evening.

"It's a military word," Jason said under his breath so Dick couldn't hear. "I read it in a book somewhere. It means you're checking out the enemy movements."

"Have you found anything?" Gudrin asked. She had slept all afternoon and looked better, William thought.

"Nothing so far."

"Something will happen tonight," she said.

"How do you know?" Jason asked.

She shrugged.

"Gudrin knows things," said Tolliver. "She always has."

"What are you children whispering about?" Dick cried from his end of the table. "I've never seen such glum faces. Come and join me in the courtyard. I long for a turn around in the fresh air to settle my stomach after this healthy repast."

William pulled Gudrin aside. "If you really think something will happen tonight, then we should take turns on the watch."

She nodded. "You and I can take the first and Jason

and Tolliver the second. Tell them we shall wake them at the third hour of the morning.''

The night was dark.

''I miss electricity,'' William said to Gudrin as they strolled back and forth along the ramparts.

''What is elec— Whatever?''

''Something that was invented about six hundred years from now. It's like that flashlight you used in the boat but electricity comes through wires in the walls. Instead of candles, you pull a switch and a light comes on.'' William looked out over the fields. ''The darkness is so black here,'' he said. ''Back where I live, even when you don't have your lights on, somebody else does, and the whole world seems brighter.''

They nodded to Alan as they passed the main gatehouse. He had been assigned by Brian to the first watch of the night, and he seemed mystified and a little put out by their appearance.

Gudrin liked carrying the binoculars, so William let her. Every so often she set both elbows on the turreted edge of the wall walk and swept the landscape from left to right, always ending with a long look at the road leading up from the coast. This time she spotted something.

''What is it?'' William asked impatiently.

''A horse walking slowly. No saddle. There is a

sack slung across its back. No, wait. It's not a sack, it's a person.''

She gave him the binoculars.

"It's a man, dressed very poorly,'' William reported to her as they made their way back toward Alan. "A peasant, I guess, and his clothes are hanging in tatters. He's lifting his head, now he's dropped it again. He must be very tired or ill. The horse looks in pretty bad shape too. I can't see much more. It's too dark.''

"If he carries the milk sickness, we must not let him into the castle,'' she warned.

"But he's come for help,'' William said. "We have to do something.''

The horse stopped on the other side of the moat and dropped its head to nibble in the sparse grass. The rider struggled to a sitting position and called out, "Hallo. Open the gates.''

"Your name, sir?'' William called.

"What matters my name when I have only hours to live. I have come as a warning. Lower the drawbridge.'' He collapsed once more against the steed's bony neck and looked as if he might never move again.

"Do it,'' William said to Alan.

"But, sir, we know not if he is an enemy.''

"You heard him. If he is, he certainly cannot harm us now. But keep an eye on the road behind him to be sure he has not been sent out as a diversion.''

William and Gudrin pounded down the twisting tower steps. Through the thick walls, they could hear the grinding and clanking of chains as the drawbridge was lowered and the portcullis raised.

Alan called orders, and two guards with torches materialized on either side of Gudrin and William as they waited in the courtyard. Then William heard Dick's voice behind him and the hushed mutterings of a gathering crowd. He didn't turn around because he couldn't drag his eyes away from what was coming across the drawbridge.

Both horse and man were bleeding from what seemed like a thousand bites. It was a wonder that anybody, animal or human, could go on walking and breathing with so much blood running from their wounds. The horse swayed to a stop and then looked as if it might fall over.

"Get the man down," Dick ordered as he pushed his way past William. Two more guards rushed forward to obey him. The crowd parted and hurried to make a bed for the man by piling up their cloaks and woolen wraps.

"It's the fisherman," Gudrin whispered to William. "The one who told us the ship had come back."

As William knelt beside the dying man, he could see that she was right. It was difficult to recognize the face because of the bites in his right cheek and above his eyebrow. William stripped off the man's shirt and as gently as possible, he pressed it against the face wounds. Gasps of horror ran through the crowd.

"Stand back," Dick said. "Give them room."

"It's you," the man croaked in a hoarse voice as he grabbed William's sleeve and pulled him closer. There was a surprising amount of strength left in his arms, perhaps from all his years of hauling nets. "You know about the death ship, don't you? You and that girl."

"Yes," William said. "What is it?"

"They come in the night," he whispered. "They eat everything alive. People, dogs, horses. Everything with flesh on it. So many of them crawling. Everywhere." He closed his eyes as if that might take the horror of the memory away.

"The rats," William said in a low voice.

"You wake up and they are already on you, on the babies," he muttered with his eyes still closed.

"Quiet, now." Gudrin had knelt down on his other side. "I have something to ease the pain but we shall have to move you." Someone had run for a woolen covering and she tucked it around him. Then she directed the guards to slide a piece of board underneath his body so that he could be moved.

"Where shall we take him, Miss Gudrin?" Brian asked.

"To my bedchamber. We are fortunate it is close to

the buttery," she said. "Gareth, boil water for me," she called out to one of the scullion boys who was standing at the edge of the crowd. He ran to do her bidding.

As the man's face rose slowly from the ground, he opened his eyes again and stared directly at William. "I came to warn you," he said. "They're headed this way."

"We'll be safe in the castle," William said. "With the drawbridge up, we'll be safe."

"They swim," the fisherman said. "They tunnel. They climb. They gnaw through anything. So many of them. Nothing stops them, I'm telling you. Nothing. They follow the leader. The big one. They watch him all the time."

"How much time do we have?" William said as he strode along beside the makeshift stretcher.

"A day at the most. Maybe two." Then the fisherman's head rolled back and he said nothing more.

CHAPTER 13

Jason found William in the courtyard after the fisherman had been borne away.

"I almost puked when I saw that," Jason said. "How could you stand to get so close to him with all that blood?"

"I don't know," William said. "Somebody had to try and do something. He told me the rats are headed this way."

"Boys, I want you to meet with me in the tower room," Dick ordered as he brushed past them. "Immediately. Brian," he called out as he strode away.

"The general commands," muttered Jason. "And we obey. What are we going to do?"

"I don't know," said William. "But we'd better make up our minds pretty soon. I don't think we have much more time."

They trudged up the tower steps, Brian and Dick ahead of them.

"This place is so dark," Jason said. "It gives me the creeps."

"It is the middle of the night," William replied. Whenever Jason was nervous, he filled the silences with chatter and William found it hard to pay attention to him. A hundred thoughts were running through his brain at the same time. What was Gudrin doing with the bleeding fisherman? Where were the rats now? What if Deegan never brought the token back? How would he and Jason get home? He closed his eyes for a moment and let his feet feel their way up the steps. Home. His soft bed, a heated house, lights at the flick of a switch. He missed all the comforts of the twentieth century. And most of all he missed his parents who were frozen in their own time, not missing him because they didn't even know he was gone.

"Now, gentlemen," Dick said when they were assembled in his room. "I have gathered you together to make a plan for the defense of the people and Sir Simon's castle. That poor man has suffered some hideous torment that seems beyond imagining. Young William, it is the rats you told me about, isn't it?"

"Yes, Dick, the ones we saw coming off the ship. They are headed this way. He says they eat everything alive, everything with flesh on it."

"But, sir," Brian said. "Rats do not normally behave this way. They are not carnivores. They serve us well by ridding us of our offal.''

"These rats are led by a huge one," Jason said. "We saw it. It's taller than Dick. It must have them under some kind of control.''

"That's why we saw the garbage and the bones floating in the river," William blurted out. "The rats are acting abnormally, like crazed cannibals.''

Dick put up his hands. "Where are they now?''

"Traveling along the road from the coast. The fisherman came to warn us. He says we have a day, two at the most, before they reach us.''

"Let me think," Dick said. They stood in silence while he took one turn about the room and then another. The cat followed him, curling in and out of his legs as he walked. He stopped and turned to face them again. "My plan is twofold," he announced in a solemn voice. "First, everybody who can, must leave. We will give them the horses and as many provisions as we can spare. A small number of us will remain behind as a decoy for these vermin. We will defend the castle until the end.'' He took a deep breath and his voice dropped to a hoarse whisper. "I would hope that the three of you will choose to stand beside me in this desperate hour but each of you must speak for yourself.''

"I am at your disposal, sir," Brian said.

"You mean you want us to be the bait for them?" Jason asked.

"In a manner of speaking. We must distract them, hold them here, so the others can get away."

Jason frowned. "How are we going to do that?"

Dick faltered. "I'm not exactly sure, young man. That is what we must work out here."

"How many are in the castle now?" William asked.

Brian cocked his head. "With the children and the stable hands, some seventy or so."

"Let me think out loud for a minute," William said. "A crowd of people that size will move slowly. Even if they take the horses, many of them will have to walk. And of course, as they travel through the countryside, others will join them and slow them down even more. The rats will overtake them soon enough. So, I agree with Dick. We have to distract the rats, lure them away. The question is how do we do that and manage to stay alive at the same time?"

"Nice of you to think of that," Jason said.

"Young Jason," Dick said sternly. "I would remind you of the trust Sir Simon left you in the form of his sword."

Jason looked embarrassed. "I know, sir. I stand ready to fight with the bravest of them."

William cut in. "I do not mean any disrespect, Dick, but what will swords do against a plague of rats?"

A frown crossed Dick's face and his shoulders sagged suddenly.

"No," William went on, his mind racing. "We must trap them in here. Lure them in and haul up the drawbridge."

"Then what?" Jason asked.

"Find a place in the castle to wait out a siege." William snapped his fingers. "We need a plan of the castle."

"In Sir Simon's bedchamber," Brian said, picking up a candle. "I will go for it."

"Good," William said. "We also need somebody to bring back Sir Simon and Deegan with the token."

Dick looked bewildered. "The token?"

"You remember, Dick," William said impatiently. "The one I snatched from Alastor. One side shrinks people and the other side makes them big again. Deegan stole it from me when he went off with Sir Simon. If we get it back, we can shrink the rats with it."

"Brilliant plan," Dick said, brightening suddenly. It was clear that he hadn't thought much beyond the diversionary tactic.

"I'll go," Jason said. "On my bike."

William studied him. "Not a bad idea. A bicycle wouldn't leave a scent the way a horse would. And you're the obvious one because you've got the most endurance on the bicycle. But you don't know the way. And frankly, we need you here."

"Are you thinking what I'm thinking?" Jason asked.

"Tolliver," William said softly.

"Exactly."

"No, he's only a boy," Dick cried.

"Listen to me, Dick, it would get him away to safety."

"And he rides really well now," Jason added. "I've been training him ever since we got here, Dick. His legs are almost as strong as mine."

"Yes," William said. "And he is a brave boy. You have taught him well. He knows the way to Inglewich. If he were to leave in the next few hours, by morning he would have put many miles between him and the—" he paused, "—and what's coming."

Dick sank onto the bench wearily. "So much to think about," he said. "I want Gudrin to go with the rest of them."

"I'm not leaving you, Uncle," said a clear voice from the doorway. They whirled around. Gudrin was standing at the top of the steps with a candle in her hand. The flickering light picked up the dark hollows under her eyes and the patches of dried brown blood that stained her skirts. She looked like a ghostly visitor from another world. "I have lost my mother, aunt, and grandmother," she said. "I will not leave you, Uncle."

"Gudrin, you are not to disobey me," Dick said,

but his weak voice betrayed him. How could he bear to have both his son and niece leave him now? William wondered. Besides, he wanted Gudrin to stay.

"We will need her," he said. Gudrin looked at him with a mixture of surprise and relief.

"The fisherman died a few minutes ago," she said, her chin raised and her voice still clear. "But I was able to ease his pain. With the poultices. Grandmother taught me well."

"Your grandmother did know what was upon us, did she not?" Dick said, his eyes raised to Gudrin's. "And I paid her no mind, I treated her like a bad child." A shudder ran through his whole body and he put his head in his hands.

Gudrin slipped onto the bench next to her uncle and put her arm around his shaking shoulders.

When Brian came back with the castle plans, William spread them out on Dick's table and stared at them for a long time in the flickering light of the candles.

"We need to get from the wall walk to the dungeon without crossing the courtyard," he said to Brian. "These stairs by the northeast tower, are they still usable?"

"Yes. Sir Simon sealed off the lower doors in that tower some years ago, but they could be reopened. The staircase comes out just between the well and the armory. Here," Brian said, pointing with his thick finger. "In this corner of the courtyard."

"And the dungeon is next to the armory?"

"Yes."

"Good. Once the rats are all in, two of us will raise the drawbridge and make a dash for the dungeon where the rest of us will be stationed with enough provisions to wait out the siege."

"It's a daring plan," Brian said. "Trap your enemy and then go into hiding."

"But will it work?" Jason asked.

"Who knows?" Gudrin said. "For the moment, it seems to be the only plan we've got."

Dick stood up. "Ring the bell," he said to Brian. "Wake everybody and order them into the courtyard. They must get on the road and away from here as soon as possible. Gudrin, you are in charge of the buttery and the division of the stores. Brian, get two of your guards to bury the fisherman and his horse in the field outside the castle walls. Then I want the carpenters to move the bar from the outside of the dungeon door to the inside. Boys, you are to prepare Tolliver for his journey. Hurry, all of you. We don't have much time." That sounds like the old Dick, William thought as the group scattered to carry out their assignments.

They found Tolliver riding circles around the courtyard on William's bicycle.

"I know it's the middle of the night, but I couldn't sleep," he called out as he swept past the first time. "I thought I'd get in some night training with the bike light."

"Save your strength," Jason said as Tolliver pulled up panting. "You're going to need it."

"My father said I could go?" asked Tolliver when he'd heard the plan.

"He agreed that you are the one who must go," William said, lying a little. "You know the way, and with all the training you've gone through, you have the muscles we need. Pretend it's a race, Tolliver. Just get there as fast as you can and send Sir Simon and Deegan back with the token. It's our only hope."

"I shall not disappoint you, Sir William, I warrant you that." Such a big speech, William thought. It scared him to think their entire plan depended on this one boy's courage and his leg muscles. What if he didn't come back? What would they do then? He shook his head as if to throw off the bad thoughts. He couldn't afford to think too far ahead.

He found Dick in a corner of the courtyard, issuing orders to the guards. "Tolliver will be ready soon," William said. "I am sure he will want your blessing on his journey."

Dick saluted him. "I am coming now."

Up above, the chapel bell began to toll—an eerie

insistent warning in the black night. William wondered if the rats could hear it as they made their way up the road from the coast.

All through the night, the courtyard was abuzz with activity. Under Gudrin's sharply delivered orders, the scullion boys ran frantically between the buttery and the stables where the horses were being prepared for the journey. People packed their meager household belongings into burlap sacks and slung them over the backs of the restless horses. The children were stirred out of their sleep and carried into the center of the courtyard where they were propped up against each other to await the departure. The younger ones toppled over and fell asleep again while the older ones watched the chaotic comings and goings in amazement. Nothing like this had ever happened before in the castle.

Soon after sunrise, the caravan was ready. Dick appointed Alan, the second-in-command under Brian, to lead the refugees. He was quite distressed at being sent off with such a raggle-taggle band of civilians, but Dick and Brian were firm with him.

"Go all the way to the border of Inglewich," Dick told him. "Tell whoever you meet that they must take what they can carry and follow you. Move the group along as fast as you can. We do not know how long we shall be able to hold this pack of vermin in the castle."

"Should you meet Sir Simon coming back this way," Brian said, "I give you permission to return with him and fight as becomes your station."

"Thank you, my liege," said Alan. "This feels a most unseemly job for a soldier," he added, looking over the crowd of crying babies and stamping horses.

"If we have managed to defeat the rats, we will hoist the Hargrave pennant at the top of the north tower," William added.

"And if there is no pennant?"

"Blow a horn three times and then storm the castle," Dick said in a low voice. "God alone knows what you will find in here by then."

Brian and Alan saluted one another. Then Brian turned sharply on his heel and marched off with Jason to raise the portcullis and lower the drawbridge. With a command, Alan stirred the people to their feet, and slowly, the unruly group began to make its way across the drawbridge. Two guards herded the final stragglers along. William stood and watched until they turned the corner. All that was left were the pink rays of early morning sunshine sliding into the corners of the dark courtyard. Then with a great clanking of the chains, the drawbridge was raised again.

William found Gudrin sorting provisions in the dungeon. It looked as if she had thought of everything.

Water had been drawn from the well and stood about in heavy wooden buckets. The stone floor was covered with hay and sweet-smelling herbs, and five pallets were spread out in a row. William realized suddenly how exhausted he was. He longed to lie down and sleep but there was work still to be done.

"What's all this?" he asked, pointing to a pile of armor and a shield.

"Jason's idea," she said. "He brought those things in from the armory. And his precious bicycle. It's over there in the corner."

"I don't know what a rat could possibly do to a bicycle," said William. "Although maybe the big one would try to ride it. Who knows? It may come in handy. What else do you need?"

"It will be dark down here all the time," she said. "Bring me four of the wall torches from up above. And warm coverings for the pallets." She looked around. "Dungeons were not built for comfort."

"At least this is strong," he said as he pulled the heavy wooden door toward him. "And I'm glad it has the window at the top because I hate being closed into spaces."

"I brought Calendar's cat down here," Gudrin said. "Seems more use than a bicycle against a horde of rats."

"Don't get on Jason's case," he warned. "We're

all going to be living in a pretty tight space for a while.''

She didn't answer, so he went away to carry out her requests.

By midafternoon, their preparations were complete and Dick said they should all try to rest. ''We will get precious little sleep in the hours to come,'' he said.

''Do we dare sleep now?'' Brian asked.

''The fisherman said they come at night,'' William said. ''So by sundown, we must be ready on the ramparts.''

Without any further discussion, they each took a pallet.

''I can't ever sleep during the day,'' Jason said into the air.

''Don't worry,'' said William. ''Even with the torches, it feels like night down here.''

And those were the last words anybody spoke for some time.

CHAPTER 14

They ate supper in the courtyard. When William saw the amount of food Gudrin had prepared for them, he wondered if she had slept at all.

"I'm starving," Jason said as he settled down. "I don't even care what this stuff is."

When they had finished eating, Dick ordered them to leave the remains of the food on the table. "Some tempting morsels for the vermin," he said.

"But, Dick, I thought we were supposed to be the tempting morsels," Jason said. "I hope these rats don't choose some dried-up old figs and boars' ears over me. I've gone to a lot of trouble to develop these muscles," he added, slapping his thighs.

"I wouldn't want to have to chew on those legs," William said. "They've been exercised into pieces of tasteless gristle."

"After all the tumbling you've done, your muscles wouldn't exactly be my idea of dinner either," Jason said, leaning over and grabbing William's upper arms. "Like chewing on leather. And what about Brian's hamstrings? After a life of horseback riding and marching. No, thank you. A piece of flesh like that might drive a self-respecting rat right back to the glories of garbage."

Brian grinned into his tankard. Gudrin was laughing so hard that the tears began to run down her face, and finally even Dick had to smile.

Gallows humor, William thought. He'd read the phrase somewhere in a book and now he knew what it meant. He looked up at the sky. The light was fading and so was their laughter. It was time.

"Brian and I will take the first shift," Dick said. "You three are to go down in the dungeon and wait for us."

They all shook their heads.

"I order it," Dick said.

They shook their heads again.

"We'll wait on the wall walk with you," William said. "As soon as we see something coming, we'll go down."

"That's right, Uncle," Gudrin said. "None of us wants to be locked up in the dungeon any longer than we have to."

Dick looked at Brian.

"We will have plenty of warning," the captain said. "They might as well come up with us. Even with William's binoculars, we could use their young eyes."

"I don't know what use I am, giving a lot of orders that nobody obeys," Dick said grumpily. "Well, come on then, the lot of you."

Gudrin slipped her arm through her uncle's. Jason and William took up positions on either side of Brian. The small but determined force made its way to the ramparts.

They spread out along the two sides of the wall walk that faced the southeast. Brian, who was stationed in the tower that looked directly onto the road, kept the binoculars. Occasionally someone would call for them, and the others would hold their posts tensely, waiting for news. The night was curiously quiet, and William hated how loudly their cries sounded in the stillness. He felt as if he were with the rats tramping up the road with their ears cocked for human voices.

Scudding clouds covered the moon. He kept one eye on Gudrin and one on the road. She would know before the rest of them when danger was coming. It was hard to see her, and he wished for more light and then changed his mind. If he could see more clearly, then so could the rats.

Gudrin said his name, once, quietly, insistently.

"What?" he called back.

"They're coming," she said. "I can hear them now."

He sucked in his breath and listened. Nothing. Not a birdcall or a rolling pebble or the rustle of a tree branch. She must have the hearing of a dog.

"Warn the others," she said. "Quietly."

He left his post and tiptoed up to her. "You're sure?" he asked.

"Positive," she said. "Go now. Hurry."

William went from Jason and Brian to Dick and they gathered around Gudrin.

"Any minute now," she said. "Down there between the trees where the road dips. That's where we'll see them first."

Brian handed William the binoculars and he focused them on the spot she had described. A minute went by, maybe two, and then he saw the first shadow of movement against the pale surface of the road. Suddenly the road was filled with dark moving shapes.

"They're walking upright," he reported in a horrified whisper. "On their hind legs. In formation. Like soldiers in a battalion. I can only see a couple of lines at a time because of the trees. There's the big one in the middle. Now he's gone."

Jason had trotted a little ways down the walk. "I see them from here," he called. "They're coming pretty fast now. There are so many of them. Like a long fat moving snake.''

Dick stared. ''I had no idea what—'' he whispered and then his voice dropped to silence.

Brian stirred himself. ''Sir, we must take our positions.''

Dick didn't answer.

William glanced over the wall again. ''Look, they've reached the fork in the road.''

The first line of rat soldiers drew to a stop and waited for instructions. The ranks parted as their leader made his way to the front. For a long time, he stood without moving and stared down the road. Suddenly, the moon came out from behind the clouds and the whole scene was tinged with a wash of silver light.

''This way,'' William whispered. ''You want to come this way.'' Out of the corner of his eye, he saw Gudrin move, and before anyone could stop her, she had leapt onto the opening between two merlons. She began to sing in a high clear voice. It was some song she must have learned at the convent and there seemed to be no particular tune but her voice rose and fell in a gentle roll.

''*O let the earth bless the Lord,*
O ye mountains and hills, bless ye the Lord,
O all ye green things upon the earth, bless ye the Lord,
Praise him and magnify him forever.''

She sang about the whales and the beasts and the cattle and the seas and the floods and she called on them to bless and magnify the Lord, and while she sang, the monster rat turned first his head and then his body toward her. As he turned, his soldiers turned too, and with a nod from their leader, they began to advance on the castle.

"That's it," William cried, pulling on her skirts. "You got them. Now come down."

When they helped Gudrin from her post, she turned and looked at William with wide glazed eyes as if she were in some kind of trance. It was the same look she had given him when he had dragged her up onto the overturned dory, and for a moment, he was tempted to slap her.

"Gudrin, listen to me," he shouted. "You've got them now! They're headed this way. Now, wake up. We need you."

She looked startled and then sorry. "I'm ready," she said in a calm voice. "What is it?"

"Your uncle. I think he's in shock. He's no use to us like this."

"Uncle," Gudrin said. She shook his shoulder. Dick went on mumbling to himself and counting some invisible threads in his tunic.

"Jason, you and Gudrin take him down to the dungeon," William said. The strength in his voice surprised even him. It was as if somebody else were speaking for him. "Hurry. I will take his place at the drawbridge. Go, now."

"Will you be all right?" she asked.

"Yes!" he screamed. "For God's sake, just get him moving. We have no more time."

Jason and Gudrin stationed themselves on either side of Dick and led him away. Once or twice he dug his heels in and tried to turn around, but they kept him moving, Gudrin whispering encouragement in his ear all the while.

William and Brian ran for the gatehouse. Once inside, they each grabbed a chain and watched through the arrow loop in the wall. The rat army flowed over the crest of the hill like a great black oil spill, marching evenly, in formation, making subtle direction shifts as the road turned with no apparent signal from their leader.

With one hand still on the chain, William picked the binoculars up from around his neck and watched as they drew closer. "They look like robots on remote control," he muttered to Brian.

"Pardon?" Brian said.

Of course Brian didn't know what a robot was. "I mean how does the leader communicate with them?" William said.

"Animals have their ways," Brian replied.

William kept the binoculars trained on the leader until the monster rat passed out of sight under the gatehouse arch. Then he switched it to the followers and saw in their eyes the same dazed, powerless look that he had noticed in the movement of their limbs. Rats scurrying around with their noses to the floor were creepy enough, but these half-human rodents marching to some unheard tune scared him even more.

"He must have some strange power over them."

"There's the end of them," Brian warned. "Just coming over the hill. Get ready." In the distance, they saw the surface of the road again as the final wave of the long, black rat river rolled up toward them.

"No sound," William whispered. "On the drawbridge. No hoofbeats, drums, people marching."

"Reach your hand as far up the chain as you can," Brian said in a steady voice. "We want to raise the drawbridge swiftly with as little warning as possible. Trap them before they even know it's happening. I'll give the signal."

William dropped the binoculars and took a deep breath. His heart was banging inside his chest the way it did just before a gymnastics meet. He tried to still it, taking the air in deeply, letting it out just as evenly, listening for the count from Brian.

"Come on," Brian said in a low, teasing voice. "Good boys, follow the leader. There you go. One, two, three, PULL, BOY, PULL WITH ALL YOU'VE GOT!'' he roared, and neither one of them cared anymore who heard them as they hauled on the chains.

Once the drawbridge was up, they secured it and crept out along the wall walk to the northeast tower. William was dying to peek over the edge into the courtyard, but he kept his head down. They stood for a moment behind the thick wooden door at the bottom of the tower steps to gather their strength.

''When we come out, we'll be just behind the well,'' Brian whispered. ''Then duck through the side door to the armory. It's a short distance from there to the dungeon. You go first and I'll cover your back. Ready?''

William nodded. Would he ever be ready for this? ''Ready,'' he said.

The moment they pulled the door open and tried to run, they were fighting their way through a moving sea of black bodies. With every step, William felt the soft furry mounds under his feet, snapping at his pants, scurrying across his sneakers. He stopped every so often to knock the bodies off his legs, but their teeth were sharp and once he felt the pain of a puncture. At the door to the armory, he looked back. Ever the soldier, Brian had stopped and turned to face the advancing enemy with his sword. The rats easily avoided the slashing blade, ducking past it time and time again to sink in their teeth.

Suddenly, the huge rat started for Brian. William saw the rear ranks part to let him through. The more the guard lashed out with the sword, the more frenzied the rats became in their attack. They were crawling over each other to get to him. And still the huge rat advanced, intent on his prey. He turned his gaze on the man, and when their eyes met, a strange stillness settled over Brian. He froze in position and dropped his sword. His will to fight was being drained away by something in the rat's eyes.

"NO!" William roared, and he threw himself at the squirming mass to get back to Brian. He shielded the man's eyes with his hands and Brian trembled as if released from some spell.

"Now, run," screamed William. "For the armory door. I'll cover you."

The monster rat had turned its attention on William, but before it could get any closer, William dropped into a series of whirling handsprings that threw the rats hanging onto his legs into space. The rest of the animals retreated in confusion.

William gauged the distance close enough, and when he came up from his last turn, he bumped into Brian who had just made it to the armory door. The two of them lurched through the dark space toward the dungeon.

Jason was waiting for them. He shoved the door open just far enough to let them through. Brian stumbled into the room and collapsed on the floor. William backed in right behind him with one last futile kick at the surge of rats chasing at his heels.

The next few moments were filled with confusion. With screams of horror and rage, Jason and Gudrin beat uselessly at the three furry bodies that had managed to slip through the door and into the room. Finally, Jason snatched up a shield and slammed it down on two of the bodies at once. The third disappeared into the dark recesses of the dungeon behind them.

"Is that all of them?" William gasped as he sank to the floor.

Jason lifted the shield slowly and looked at the flattened bodies. He kicked them aside in disgust. "One got away," he muttered. "It's in here with us somewhere."

Gudrin dropped to her knees beside Brian. She tried to stop the flow of blood from his legs with her skirts.

"Are you all right?" Jason asked.

William didn't answer.

"Your leg is bleeding," Jason said. "Come on, I'll help you get your pants off."

William lay down and allowed Jason to strip off his jeans. He didn't even care whether Gudrin saw him half naked.

"It's not too bad," Jason said. "Just one small bite above the ankle."

"It's throbbing," William whispered. He felt somebody wrap a warm wet dressing on the place where it
hurt. The pain shot up his leg, but it felt oddly distant,
as if his leg and his wound belonged to another person.
He felt nothing more for a long time.

CHAPTER 15

He heard a voice first. Then something moved through his hair, and with a cry, he struggled to a sitting position.

"It's all right," Gudrin whispered to him. "It's only me. How are you?"

"My leg hurts," he said.

"I've brought you something to drink," she said, and he let her put the tankard to his mouth. When he tried to turn his face away after the first bitter swallow, she took his chin in her hand and made him take the rest.

"Yuk," he spluttered. "What was that?"

"Something for the pain. It will make you sleep again. I've put a dressing on the bite. Sorrel and mustard root. It will speed the healing."

"Brian?" he asked.

"Resting for now." It must be pretty bad, he thought.

"The rats?"

"We're safe in here," she whispered with her mouth close to his ear. "Calendar's cat got the last one. Hush, now."

When he slid down to the pallet, she sang to him, a soft little tune about the sky, and he let the words wash over him and then he slept again.

He woke later to a scraping noise, like someone digging a tunnel.

"What's that?" he said into the air.

"The rats," Gudrin's voice answered him from across the room. "They're gnawing on the door."

He propped himself up and looked around. She was sitting on a bench against the wall, stripping leaves off some weedy-looking plants. Brian was snoring gently on his pallet and Dick was walking in tight circles in the darker recesses of the room.

"Jason," William called.

"Right here," Jason said from his perch under one of the torches. He was sorting through his pile of armor.

"What time is it?" William asked.

Jason consulted his watch. "Three in the afternoon, I think. It's easy to lose track down here."

"So how long have I been asleep?"

"One full night," Gudrin said. "And half of another day."

William struggled to his feet and tested his leg. A sharp pain shot up through the muscles, but once he rested his full weight on it, the pain turned into a dull throb.

He shot Jason a desperate look. "Where do we—"

Jason pointed over his shoulder with his thumb. "Go around the corner. There's a garderobe. I'm sure our jails at home don't have such nice bathrooms," he added with a grin.

On the way back, William stopped and looked into Brian's face. The man was still asleep, taking in air in ragged, uneven breaths. Wet dressings covered most of his legs, which Gudrin had left exposed to the air.

"Brave man," William whispered to his comrade.

"He's got two bites on his stomach," Jason said. "They must have crawled in under the chain mail shirt."

"He should have run the way I did, but he turned to fight them," William said. "They were all over him when I went back."

He limped over to the bench and Gudrin put a trencher on his lap. Bread, figs, some dried meat. He wolfed it down. "How's the food and water holding out?"

"Not bad," Jason said. "Miss Gudrin, here, is quite the chef."

"What about Dick?"

"He just keeps walking around and around in a circle," Jason said. He glanced at Gudrin.

"He's talking to Tolliver's mother," she said quietly. A shudder ran through her thin shoulders and William decided to change the subject.

"How long has the gnawing been going on?"

"It started soon after you and Brian came in," Gudrin said. "The door is thick," she added, but her voice faltered.

The sudden silence between them made the scrabbling at the door seem even louder in the cold room.

"I hate that noise," William said, shoving his fingers into his ears.

"Get used to it, old buddy," Jason mouthed.

"Did you bring your dagger?" William asked. "The one from the castle in the attic?"

Jason produced it from the bottom of his backpack.

William grabbed the dagger and hobbled across the room. He shoved it through the crack under the door to distract the rats, but the weapon wasn't long enough. Nothing stopped the scrape of the rats' teeth against the wood. He threw the dagger away in disgust.

"I've got Sir Simon's sword if you want something longer," Jason said. "But it won't make them stop. Nothing does."

"Boost me up," William said to his friend. "I want to look through the window."

Jason shrugged. "I've already tried that too. You won't be able to see anything. It's too dark out there."

"Let me try anyway," William said.

Jason made a step with his hands, and William put his good leg into it and pushed himself up. It took a minute for his eyes to adjust to the darker room outside, but even when they did, he saw what Jason meant. The walls of the castle had been built for defense, not for light. All William could see was the vague movement of shadows in the darkness as if the floor of the room were covered with a huge undulating rug. He rested his forehead against the iron bars of the small window for a moment and fought back tears.

"Okay, let me down," he muttered to Jason, who lowered him carefully until his foot touched the floor. "I hate this," he said. "I hate being trapped in small places. It makes me crazy."

Jason and Gudrin stared at him without saying anything. He knew what they were thinking. Don't complain, old buddy, you're the one who got us into this mess.

It had sounded like such a good idea back then, but here they were, trapped in the dungeon with one wounded soldier and a man who had gone off his head and what sounded like a million rats gnawing at the door. And Gudrin and Jason were both expecting him to find a way out.

He stomped over and picked the dagger up from the floor. "We've got to keep track of time or we'll go crazy," he said as he cut one deep line in the wood of the bench. "That's for the twenty-four hours from the time Tolliver left until we got down here." He started to dig a second mark, but Jason put out a hand to stop him.

"No cheating," he said. "Ten o'clock tonight we make the next mark. Seven hours from now."

"It's only been a day and a half since Tolliver left?" William asked. "Are you sure?"

Gudrin nodded.

"Do you think he's gotten to Sir Simon yet?" asked William.

She shook her head. "It's a two-day ride to Inglewich," she said. "In the best of circumstances. And he is only a boy."

Now that the worst had happened to them, William wondered if she had any more predictions to make.

"You heard the rats coming," he said to her. "Do you hear them going away?"

"It is always difficult to hear silence," she said in a tone that seemed to mock him. William thought again of the girls he knew at home and how different she was, how much older than her twelve years. She stood up and with a swish of burlap skirts, went to tend to Brian.

Just then, the cat emerged from some dark corner and prowled along the edges of the room until he reached the door. He stopped to sniff at the thin crack along the bottom, froze and then hissed. The gnawing did not lessen; in fact it seemed to increase as he yowled in frustration. William went over and scooped him up off the floor.

"Give him some scraps of meat," Gudrin said from where she knelt over Brian. "It will distract him."

The day took forever to end. Jason polished each piece of his armor with his bicycle rag. He spent most of his time on the shield, spitting and rubbing and spitting again. Gudrin moved from Brian to her uncle. She managed to coax him to the bench where she fed him and stroked his hair and listened to his babblings. Once when William glanced at the two of them, he could see tears glistening on Gudrin's cheeks.

Everybody but William seemed to have something to do. They concentrated on their little jobs as if they didn't have a care in the world, as if the endless scraping at the door didn't concern them in the least, as if all they had to do was wait because he was going to figure a way out of this mess. It made him angry and restless. He asked the time so often that Jason finally took off his watch and tossed it across the room to him.

On the dot of ten, William carved the second line in the bench and ordered them all to bed. At least I'll act as if I'm in charge, he said to himself, as he tossed one way and then the other on the pallet. Finally, he tore two strips of cloth from the sleeves of his shirt and stuffed them in his ears to try and stop the noise.

His first thought when he woke was that the make-shift earplugs had worked and he put his fingers up to shove them in even farther. But they had fallen out during the night. What he was hearing was silence. He sat up and looked around. The others were still asleep in lumpy piles on their pallets.

It must be morning, he thought, because even though the torch above the bench had gone out during the night, the faintest ray of light had made its way into their black hole of a prison. The watch hands glowed faintly. Six-thirty A.M. And no more gnawing. Maybe they've given up, gone off to chew on some other victims. Before I wake the others, I'll just check, he thought. Ever so quietly, he upended an empty water barrel and scrambled onto it.

His eyes had grown so used to half-light, to the uncertain flicker of smoky torches, that for a moment he was almost blinded by the bright strip of sunlight that lay across the rough stones of the anteroom floor. He couldn't see its source, but he knew it must come from an arrow loop in the eastern wall of the outer room. And he also knew it wouldn't last long.

In the shadows against the opposite wall, he caught some movement, and slowly his eyes began to distinguish one shape from another. The rats were lined up in marching formation across the room, their backs against the wall, still, awaiting orders. William scanned the ranks for the leader and found him pressed into the darkest corner. What were they waiting for? What had made them stop the gnawing?

Then the leader must have given some secret signal because the first line of rats took one step forward and halted at the edge of the narrow strip of light. As the sun moved by inches across the hay-strewn cobblestone floor, the rats followed it toward the door of the dungeon. The light seemed to form some invisible boundary, and the rats did not allow so much as a whisker to be touched by it.

In time, they made it back to the door and began their gnawing again, but William stayed where he was. He waited with his face tilted downward until that first ray of sun had made its way up the side of the door to warm his skin. He opened his eyes in the white light and drank it in. As the warmth moved slowly across his face, he lifted his head to follow it and stood on his tiptoes to catch the last trickle before it slid away. He dropped down off the barrel and landed on his good leg.

Jason came around the corner from the garderobe. He stepped carefully over the sleeping bodies.

"What were you doing?" he whispered as he leaned over and pressed his finger against the rough wood.

"Watching them," William said. "There's an arrow loop at one end of the anteroom that catches the eastern sun. When I woke up, they had stopped gnawing because the sun was in the way."

"What do you mean?"

"They won't stand in the direct sunlight or get anywhere near it. Especially the leader."

Jason dropped to his knees and ran his fingers over the lower part of the door. He looked like a doctor listening to a patient's chest. Then he signaled to William to step away from it.

"It's getting weak in places," he whispered. "It's not going to last forever."

"Are you serious?" William said. "That door is two feet thick."

"Not anymore." The two of them sank down on the bench and stared at each other.

Suddenly the cat appeared from nowhere. He floated across the room to the door and sniffed along the bottom edge of it. Then he settled himself to wait, with his tail sweeping the floor in regular rhythmic strokes like the pendulum of a clock.

"He smells them getting closer," Jason said.

"Little does he know how many of them there are." William glanced down at the bench. Two and a half days had passed. Sir Simon and Deegan were just starting off from Inglewich.

"The fisherman told me the rats come at night," William said, his thoughts reeling out a little ahead of his words. "And they seem to be scared of light. So as long as we have light, we'll be okay."

"That's great," said Jason. "We're locked in the darkest room in the whole castle, and you're talking about light. Do you have any more matches in your backpack?"

"No, I already checked," William said. "All the ones we had went overboard with the dory. Plus the flashlight."

"The torches are getting low," Jason said. "Did you see the one above us has already gone out?"

"I saw," William said.

Gudrin slid onto the bench beside them. "Brian is better this morning," she said. "He's talking sense for the first time. And some of the bites have scabbed over."

"Great," William said. "We could use some good news."

"What is it?"

"The door's giving way and the torches are running out of oil," Jason said.

"We're going to have to make a break for it," William muttered, mostly to himself.

They looked at him as if he were crazy.

"Listen, you had enough trouble with that crowd out there when there were just two of you," Jason said. "Now we've got one wounded man and one guy who's crazy and a—" Jason glanced at Gudrin and stopped. "Not great odds," he finished lamely.

"Well, what do you suggest?" William asked. "Stay here until all the light is gone and the rats gnaw their way through the door and overrun us?"

"What about Sir Simon and the token?" Jason asked.

"Two and a half days have gone by. That means they're just starting back now. Do you think that door is going to last for another day and a half?"

The other two slumped into silence, but William was getting the faintest stirrings of an idea. "Listen to me," he said. "The rats are scared of light. Especially the big one. The sun lights up that room at six-fifteen in the morning for about thirty minutes. That's when we go."

"They're scared of light?" Gudrin asked, and William told her what he had seen through the barred window.

"So once we get out into the courtyard, we should be safe," Gudrin said.

"That's right. They won't follow us into the light. Particularly the big one. He was hiding in the darkest corner of the room."

"Then what?" Jason said.

"We drop the drawbridge and get out of here. We'll have the whole day to travel."

"What if it rains tomorrow?"

"Jason, I can't think of everything!" William exploded. "Come on."

"Sorry," he whispered. "I just don't think we're going to make it."

"Well, until you come up with something better, we don't have any choices."

They spent the rest of the day fine-tuning their plan. When they explained to Brian what they were going to do, he pulled himself to his feet and hobbled around the room testing his wounded legs.

"Rest, Brian," Gudrin ordered.

"I've only got a day to get myself back up to fighting strength," he said. "I'd like another crack at those nasty vermin."

"We're not going to fight them, Brian," William said. "We're just going to get away. No more noble stands, my friend."

"Yes, sir," Brian said and started on another tour of the room.

Gudrin gathered what was left of the food and packed it into the boys' two backpacks. Jason gave her his two water bottles to fill and his helmet.

"What's this for?"

"To wear on your head," he said with a shrug. "For extra protection."

"Not for me," she said. "Why aren't you wearing it?"

"Because I'm going out in the armor," Jason said in a low voice, but William heard him from across the room.

"That armor's too big for you," William said. "You won't be able to move as quickly."

"I'll go out first and beat them back with Sir Simon's sword," Jason said. He was talking in a loud, don't-tell-me-what-to-do voice.

"The light's the thing that will keep them away from us," William said.

"Listen, old buddy, you've got your ways of doing things and I've got mine," Jason said.

He's scared, William thought, and without another word, he shrugged and turned away.

Toward evening, after they had eaten, William asked Jason for the repair kit.

"What for?"

"I need to take the side mirror off your bike. I figure I can use it to deflect the sunlight. It might buy us a little more time."

"Sure, go ahead. But we're taking the bike with us."

The two of them stared at each other. "We'll come back for it later, Jason," William said gently. "It will just hold us up if we try to take it out with us tomorrow. We've got to travel light.''

"Couldn't Gudrin walk it out?''

"I'll have my hands full with my uncle,'' she said.

Jason looked from one to the other of them and his shoulders sagged. William clapped him on the back. "Cheer up,'' he said. "I promise. We'll come back for it.''

"If we get away from here, I'm never coming back,'' Jason said. "I want to get home as fast as I can,'' he added, and his voice broke.

"We're going to make it,'' William said in a voice that sounded a lot more convincing than he felt.

At ten, he made the third mark in the bench and set the alarm on Jason's watch for five-thirty in the morning. They lined up the pallets near the door and Gudrin set the backpacks next to them.

"I'll never get to sleep,'' Jason said into the air when they had all settled down.

"Sing to us, Gudrin,'' Dick said in a clear voice that startled them. Gudrin had spent the last hour telling him their plans for the morning, and he seemed more cheerful and alert than he had for days.

Gudrin sang them a song about the spring and the dawn, and the lilting tune wound its way into William's head. The next thing he heard was the tiny hammering beep of the watch alarm.

CHAPTER 16

Brian helped Jason into his armor and lowered the helmet over his head. Jason poked his finger through the opening to straighten his glasses.

"Remember one thing," William said as he slid the bike mirror into his belt. "Do not look into the big rat's eyes. He puts some weird spell on you that freezes you in your tracks. And no matter what happens, stay in the light."

"I'll go first," Jason said in a muffled voice. He looked like a kid dressed up for Halloween. "Where's my shield?"

William handed him the shield and Sir Simon's sword. "Can you see all right?"

"Sort of," Jason said. "I wish this stupid helmet would stop sliding around."

Don't wear it, William wanted to say but he kept quiet. No use starting a fight now.

Two more torches had gone out during the night. Brian was carrying the last one but it was already sputtering. They gathered in a line at the door and waited for the gnawing to stop. When it didn't, William began to doubt himself. Maybe yesterday had been a fluke. Maybe it was raining today. They had absolutely no way of knowing. Everybody began to get restless. The two men were carrying the backpacks, and they kept adjusting the straps.

"We're going no matter what," William said. "There's no use staying here."

The others murmured agreement, but nobody wanted to talk about it, about what was waiting for them on the other side of the door, or about the more certain horror of what they faced if they stayed in the dungeon. The cat curled in around Dick's legs and he leaned over to scoop the animal up.

"The light's coming," Brian said at last. He was the only one tall enough to see through the barred window. "It's getting brighter out there."

And then ever so slowly, the gnawing stopped and there was the barest scuffling sound as the hundreds of rat feet backed their way across the floor.

William lifted the bar on the inside of the door and swung it open. For a moment, nobody moved. They stood blinking in the dusty morning light. Row after row of rats faced them, on their hind legs again, upper paws resting on the shoulders of the rat in front. From behind him, William heard Dick gasp in horror.

Jason was the first to go. With a swift parry of his sword and a great clanking of metal, he marched into the anteroom. The rats did not flinch but held their ground right at the edge of the light and watched this strange creature advance toward them.

''Let's go,'' William said to the others as he pulled the mirror out of his belt. ''Follow the light right to the end wall and then make a break for the courtyard. Brian, you and Dick get away first. The three of us will follow you.'' As they filed out of the door, Gudrin came up and stood next to William while the two men slipped out and started for the end wall.

William didn't know whether Jason forgot about the light or whether the helmet slid one more time and he couldn't see. But suddenly he took another menacing step toward the line of vermin while William yelled at him to stop, to back away, to hug the light. Jason tripped on something and with a horrible, hollow cry, he stumbled and pitched forward to the ground. The helmet rolled off and there he lay with his head and neck exposed and the front half of him in the midst of a boiling dark caldron of starving rats.

Gudrin screamed, and without thinking, William

tossed her the mirror. He snatched up Jason's shiny silver shield from where it had skittered across the stone floor. Waving it wildly, he rushed to Jason's side and covered his head and neck with it.

"Get away from him!" William screamed, half out of his head with rage. And to his amazement, the rats did. They backed off again.

"It's the light," Gudrin called. "Catch the light with the shield."

With one foot on either side of Jason's body, William held up the shield with both hands so that the sun was reflected toward the rats. As they backed up, he tilted the shield ever so slightly and they retreated again. From where she stood, Gudrin held them in place with a thin shaft of mirrored light until they began to break ranks and scramble over one another in a desperate effort to get away.

"Crawl back into the light path behind me," William said to Jason, who was still lying between his legs. Jason dug his ironclad heels into the grooves between the cobblestones and with a terrible scraping noise, managed to drag himself out of danger.

With Jason safe for the moment, William lifted the shield from the ground, lost the light, and then found it again.

"Keep going," Gudrin crowed from behind him, and without turning around, he heard again that wild tumult in her voice that seemed to come from another world and reminded him of Calendar.

William took another step forward. The rats were in full retreat, rolling over each other in desperate waves, and as they went, they exposed their leader. He stood in the darkest corner of the room, his sleek hairy back pressed tightly against the stone wall.

As William advanced on the rat, he examined every detail of the monster before him. He saw the pink-tipped paws as large as human hands, the long, rope-like gray tail that curled around in front of his thick fur-covered haunches, the hairless exposed belly, and finally the face. William had never seen such a look of terror on any face, human or animal. The lips were curled away to expose long yellow teeth and the rat's eyes no longer held any power. They darted back and forth searching for an escape route but there was none.

William tipped the shield farther and the brilliant light struck the ugly leader in the eyes. From his mouth issued a long, high-pitched scream, a primitive un-earthly sound that seemed to wind like a snake out of the depths of his body.

And he began to shrivel. It did not take long. One minute he was there, and the next, he had melted down the wall like a dark stain, washed away by a stream of light. Now the size of the other rats, he was lost among them for a moment.

But suddenly, without any warning, the rat followers turned on their leader and attacked him. With a frenzied squeaking, they scrambled over one another in their rush to get at him, to sink their teeth into what was left of him. William watched in horror as they finished him off, then dropped away and scurried to and fro with their noses to the floor.

They ran across Jason's armored body as he struggled to get to his feet. He covered his face with his hands, but the animals didn't even stop to sniff at his exposed skin. The boy no longer smelled like food. He was just an obstacle lying in their way. Gudrin and Dick went back to Jason and helped him up.

"Brian, we've got to lower the drawbridge," William called. "They want out. They're nothing but rats now."

He dropped the shield, and surrounded by the surging black mass, he ran for the tower steps. The rats spilled past him into the courtyard. He heard Brian's labored breathing and saw the pain in the man's face as he stumbled up beside him into the gatehouse. Together they unlocked the chains and slowly lowered the massive wooden planking. At one point, William lost control of the drop and his feet left the ground as the chain pulled him up. He loosened his grip and let his sore fingers slide down the rough metal links until he felt solid stone once more beneath him.

The rest of them were waiting on the wall walk, hanging over the side and watching as the rats rolled out across the drawbridge. In their eagerness to flee, some of them tumbled over the edge into the moat. As soon as they surfaced, they paddled frantically through the murky water toward the opposite shore. Out on the road, they peeled off in different directions, some running toward the coast and others taking refuge in the high grass of the fields.

"So many of them," Dick said in wonder. "Who would have thought there were this many rats in the world?"

"I think that's the last of them," Gudrin said as the final stragglers scuttled off down the road. "Whatever the cat didn't get."

"Will anybody believe us when we tell them what we've seen?" Brian wondered out loud.

"We can show them the door," Gudrin said in a quiet voice.

"Was it bad?" William asked, catching her eye.

"We had an hour left, two at the most."

"We must raise the pennant from the north tower," Jason said.

"Later," said William.

Jason had managed to take off most of the armor and he looked peculiar standing there in a metal breastplate and lycra shorts. Half-knight, half-bicyclist, William thought.

"Thanks," Jason said in a low voice.

"Sure," said William with a casual shrug because he knew how hard it must have been for Jason to say that one word.

Nobody said anything more for a long time. The sun had climbed far enough above the horizon that its rays hit them full in the face. They stood in a scraggly row, soaking up its warmth.

CHAPTER 17

They slept for the rest of that day and most of the next. William and Jason were on the wall walk standing the watch when they heard the distant call of a horn.

"Someone's coming," Jason said. He was pacing back and forth with his backpack over his shoulder.

"Sir Simon," William said as Moonlight topped the hill and came thundering down the slope followed by six horsemen, riding in a tight pack.

"I hope Tolliver's with them," Jason said. "Otherwise we'll have to wait for your bike before we can leave."

William scanned the line of horses with his binoculars. "Sir Simon's there. And Alan. And the soldiers who went with him. They must have met up on the road." He put the binoculars down. "No Tolliver. No Deegan."

"Blast," said Jason and began to pace again.

The boys waited until the horses drew up at the edge of the moat. Sir Simon lifted off his helmet and rested it in his lap.

"Sir Simon of Hargrave, recently returned with some honor from Inglewich, sends his greetings to your noble selves."

"And ours to you, Sir Simon," William called back.

"It seems that you have vanquished the enemy, my good lord," Sir Simon said.

"That we have done. But we are right glad to see you."

"The Silver Knight humbly begs permission to enter," Sir Simon said with a grin.

"Permission granted," William said.

"Why didn't you ask him about Deegan?" Jason said as they trotted along the wall walk to the gatehouse.

"In time," William said. "Sir Simon loves ceremony. It's better not to rush him."

Down in the courtyard, there ensued a great clamor of greetings and hurrahs, bear hugs and a general clapping of backs and shoulders. When the horses had been led away to the stables, Sir Simon took William aside.

"You have seen much, my boy."

"Yes," William said. There is no sign of what has gone on here, he thought as he looked around the courtyard.

"Tell me about it," Sir Simon said.

William nodded. "Come to the dungeon with me. It's easier to show you."

Once William had finished the story, Sir Simon hunkered down next to the dungeon door and ran his fingers across the jagged teeth marks. At one place near the hinge, he pushed too hard and his hand went through.

"I had no idea," he said as he stood up. "No idea what you would be facing. It was wrong of me. I was warned but I chose to ignore the omens."

William said nothing. The man was right. He had been warned.

"A monstrous rat who fed on darkness," Sir Simon mused out loud. "Why? Where did he come from? Will there be another?"

"Keep Gudrin close to you," William said simply. "She will know just the way Calendar must have. They see and hear things before they happen."

Sir Simon smiled. "Oh dear, it is not fitting for a strong and fearless knight to make his apologies to an unruly girl, but I expect I shall have to."

"Yes," William said. "I expect you will."

"For the second time, I have you to thank, young William. If you had not been here, I tremble to think what we would have found when we returned. First Alastor and now this."

William stood still and let the words wash over him.

"I suppose you wouldn't consider staying here with us, my boy? I am growing old and could use your courage and your sharp wits by my side."

William shook his head. "You shall have Tolliver, my lord. He is showing much promise."

"Yes, a fine boy. Strong legs. He made good time on that contraption of yours."

"When do you think he'll be back?" William asked.

"Tomorrow. He turned right around and came back with us, but I had to leave him at the house of a friendly farmer last night. He was bone-tired and could no longer keep up."

"And Deegan?" William whispered, terrified of the answer.

"He was with us when we started out but he slipped away the afternoon of the second day. Such an irritating fool, he is. Not to be trusted."

"No," William said, close to tears. Would he and Jason ever get away from here? More than anything else at that moment, he longed for the familiar smells of his own kitchen before dinner, the sight of his father lying on the couch in the living room listening to one of his favorite operas. He desperately wanted his life to be normal again.

"Don't look so sad," Sir Simon said, clapping him on the shoulder a little too roughly. "Deegan will return in his own time. He always does. Now I must go along and have a word with Dick and Brian."

He stole the token from me, William wanted to say, but he couldn't stand to hear his own voice speaking the words out loud.

William woke in the middle of the night to find Deegan tucking something under his pallet. He reached out and grabbed the man's thin wrist.

"Deegan," he whispered so as not to wake Jason.

"The very one," whispered the fool.

"You brought it back."

William felt the fool press the token into his open palm and close his fingers over it.

"Outside," William said. "I want to talk to you."

They stood facing each other in the torchlight of the hallway and neither said anything for a while. Finally Deegan put up his fists.

"You wish to fight the fool?"

William shook his head.

Deegan stood on his hands. "Outtumble him?" he called with his face near the floor.

William shook his head again. "Stop fooling around," he muttered.

Deegan laughed as he righted himself. "You're asking a fool to stop fooling around? Seems most bizarre. It is my calling in life."

"You stole the token from me," William said. "You betrayed me. You left us with no weapon."

"Of the others I cannot speak, but you have weapons of your own," said Deegan. "From the tales Miss Gudrin tells me, they served you far better than all the swords and breastplates in the armory."

"The token would have been a lot faster and easier," William said.

"The token suited my purposes perfectly," Deegan said. "It serves as a weapon only for the likes of me, a half-boy, half-man. You were ready to cross over. The token would have held you back. And remember that a fool is not—"

"I know," William said with a shake of his head. "Not to be counted on."

Deegan bowed low. "Sir William, I do salute you and wish you a safe journey."

Before William could answer, the fool had slipped away into the dark space beyond the torchlight.

Tolliver came pedaling across the drawbridge early the next morning and they gathered around to greet him.

"I wanted to come back with them and fight," he told William in a breathless voice. "And now I hear there was no need. There is already talk of it in the countryside."

"Sir Simon tells me you rode well," William said. "We knew you would. Go, get something to eat and we'll come to say good-bye."

"But, boys, you must stay just one more night," Sir Simon roared. "I have planned a great banquet. A victory feast to celebrate your brave deeds and the defeat of the dark enemy."

Jason and William glanced at each other and shook their heads.

"We're ready to go, Sir Simon," William said.

"More than ready," added Jason, who had been riding his bicycle in frenzied circles around the courtyard since dawn.

It was decided that Tolliver and Gudrin would escort the two travelers to the edge of the forest.

"You can take my bike," William told Tolliver. "After all, where I live, I can ride a bike every day. I want to ride Mandrake one more time."

Tolliver's face lit up. "Great. That means I can race against Jason."

The small group of soldiers in the castle turned out to wish them good-bye. Jason and William went down the line, saluting each of them while Gudrin held the two horses at the ready and Tolliver balanced the bikes. When William came to Brian, the old soldier grabbed him in a crushing hug.

"I will not forget your courage," the man whispered in William's ear.

"Nor I yours," William replied.

He bowed to Dick and then shook his hand. "We did it, didn't we, Dick? We saved the castle."

"That we did," said Dick. "I will not say goodbye, young William. Only Godspeed."

When Sir Simon opened his mouth to deliver one of his speeches, William put his finger up to his old friend's lips. "Please don't," he whispered. "We've said all we need to say to one another."

Sir Simon grunted. "Except farewell, my boy. Until we meet again."

"Whenever and wherever that might be." One last time, the man's thick arms encircled William and they hugged.

William swung up onto Mandrake and settled himself into the saddle. Jason and Tolliver led the way across the drawbridge, followed by Gudrin on Sorrel. Finally, William touched his heels to his horse's thick belly and Mandrake broke into an energetic trot. For the last time, William heard the pounding of thick hooves on the planking, but he did not turn around or allow himself to look back until his horse had topped the first rise. Then he reined her in, twisted in his seat, and lifted his arm. A row of arms saluted him from the wall walk and he spurred Mandrake to a gallop to catch up with Gudrin.

When he pulled up beside her, she slowed Sorrel to a walk and nodded at the two bicyclists who were already beating their way up the next hill.

"They're determined to race," she said.

"Let them," was all William said.

They rode in a comfortable silence for quite a long time. William glanced at her once or twice, but as usual, the expression on her face was blocked by her thick hair. The two of them had barely spoken since their release from the dungeon, and he wondered how she felt about everything that had happened to them. His time with her was coming to an end and he had a million questions to ask her but at the same time he liked the silence too.

"I want to tell you about my mother," she said suddenly, still staring out at the road ahead of them. When he opened his mouth to speak, she raised her hand. "Don't talk," she said. "Just listen."

She told him about the color of her mother's hair and the songs she sang when Gudrin was a baby and the way she liked to lie down in the middle of a field with her arms spread out and stare at the sky. As Gudrin's voice rolled out in front of them, the road rolled past under their feet. William had the feeling that she wanted him to take all this away with him and hold on to it, so that on the other side of the forest in his world, there would be someone helping her with the remembering.

He listened very hard, almost as if he were taking notes for a test, and when her voice finally ran down and they had gone some distance in silence again, he said, "I won't forget anything you told me." She nodded her thanks and spoke no more about it.

William thought back on all they had gone through together.

"We're a good team," he said.

"We are?"

"Sure. If anyone needs a boat burned or a rat shrunk, they should call on us."

She put back her head and laughed, and he liked the free, silly sound of it.

"Race you," she cried, and was off before he had time to answer. He dug his heels into Mandrake and spent the rest of that wild ride trying to hang on and keep up with her at the same time.

Jason and Tolliver were waiting for them at the edge of the forest.

"Where have you been?" Jason shouted as the two horses slowed to a walk in the tall grass.

"Racing," William said.

"And I won," Gudrin said.

William shrugged. "She's right. She was ahead of me the whole way."

"I almost beat Jason," Tolliver said proudly.

"The kid's good," Jason admitted. "Of course, he's had the best trainer around."

William swung down off Mandrake and gave her a pat on the nose. "So long, old girl." He handed the reins to Tolliver and took the bike from him. They both mounted, and for a minute they all sat in a circle and looked at each other.

Jason was the first to move. "We'd better get going. Thanks, guys. Wouldn't have missed it for the world."

And then, before they could even answer, he had pushed off with one foot and was quickly swallowed up by the shadows of the forest.

"He really wants to get home," William said. "Take care of yourselves. And everybody back there."

"Will you return?" Tolliver asked.

"Who knows?" William said.

"Keep the token in a safe place," Gudrin said, looking down at him. He knew it was her way of saying, come back.

Then all at once, as if it had been planned, the three of them turned at the exact same moment and rode away from each other. William was deep into the forest before he stopped and looked back, but by that time they were out of sight. The only sign of their passing was the cloud of dust their horses had kicked up, hovering in the air above the road.

"Jason," he called out as he pushed off again. "Jason, wait up."

EPILOGUE

One Saturday morning, two weeks later, William and Jason were riding home from town when William took a right-hand turn.

"Where are we going?" Jason called, but William didn't answer until he had pulled off the road on the hill above the train station.

They stood in silence for a while with their bikes resting against their hips. In the distance a whistle blew.

"That's the ten-seventeen," Jason said. "Freight."

William scanned the side of the tracks as the engine slowed down for the station. Nobody was jumping today.

"I'm not ever going to jump the trains," William said slowly, half to himself. "It's a crazy thing to do."

Jason didn't say anything for the longest time, and William wondered what he was thinking. They watched the train until it had moved on through. Sunlight glinted off the tracks.

"Guess there's more than one way to jump the trains," Jason said to the air. He finally looked over at William. "Are they still all back there somewhere? Six hundred years away on the other side of the forest. It gives me an eerie feeling. Maybe it never happened."

"That's what I thought the first time I came back," William said. "But there are signs."

"My muscles," Jason said. He stuck one leg out and turned it this way and that to admire it. "Dad thinks I've been going out for secret training runs at night. He can't figure it out."

"And the crack in your glasses."

"Mom wasn't too happy about that."

And the letter I discovered in the bottom of my backpack when I got home, William thought. It said: "Dere Wilyem, Here are herbs for your mother the baby docter. Rue for mouth sores. Mentha for the grip and akes in the head. Be well. Gudrin." Pressed between two pages of rough paper, he found a little pile of flattened green leaves that smelled musty and ancient. He put the packet and the token in a small wooden box and took it up to the attic early one morning before the sun rose. He dropped the castle drawbridge and raised the portcullis. Then he sat in the darkness and waited for the sun to come sliding through the eastern window. It traveled across the floor toward the castle and then made its way into the courtyard where it lit up the covered passageway on the far side. He hid the box in that spot.

Jason swung his leg back over his bike. "The token?" he asked.

William nodded. "It's in a safe place. In case."

Jason grinned. "In case."

READ

The Castle in the Attic

Elizabeth Winthrop

A Yearling Book

Now available in all bookstores

ISBN: 0-440-40941-1 $5.50 U.S.
                                        $8.50 Canada

"Where did the castle come from? Tell me again," William said at dinner.

When they ate alone, they always sat in the kitchen. The checkered curtains, the yeasty smell of Mrs. Phillips's toast spread with Marmite, and the circle of light that the green shaded lamp cast around them made William feel cozy in the big, creaky house.

She did not settle into her seat until everything was in place on the table: their plates, the salt and pepper, honey for her tea, ketchup for his noodles, and chocolate syrup for his milk.

"I hate to get up in the middle of a meal," she said.

"You say that every night."

"And I mean it every night." She poured some

honey into her tea. The floating spirals of gold slipped underneath the surface, one little circle after another. "Now about the castle. Every family has its own traditions that reach back into that family's history, into another time. Other people pass on Bibles or journals or old wedding dresses. My family has always passed on the castle. It goes back as far as my father's great-grandfather and probably to before that, although we don't have certain proof of it." She took a bite and chewed on it thoughtfully. "You remember when I went back to England last year?"

William nodded, his mouth full.

"I found the castle in my parents' house when my brother Richard and I were clearing it out. That's when I had it shipped to America."

"All the way from Stow-on-the-Wold, England?" said William. He used any excuse to roll that funny name around on his tongue.

"Now all the way to Riveredge Lane, Southbrook, New York, care of William Edward Lawrence, complete with drawbridge, chapel, armory, minstrels' gallery, and one Silver Knight. The tapioca pudding is in the icebox. None for me tonight."

He cleared the table and rinsed the plates. "What about the Silver Knight?" he asked, his voice raised over the running water. "Has he always been in the castle?"

"As far as I know. I think there might have been other soldiers originally because my great-grandfather mentioned some in a letter about the castle, but I've never seen them. When I was a child, there was only the Silver Knight. There was some legend that was passed down about him. I remember bits and pieces of it. He was thrown out of his kingdom long ago by an enemy of some sort, and it's said that one day he'll come back to life and return to reclaim his land. But the whole time I played with the castle, he was as stiff and cold as lead.''

William sat down again. He made paths in his pudding with his spoon before taking the first bite. He wasn't really listening to her story. The question of her leaving hung between them. It took up as much room at the table as he did.

"Afterward," he started, his voice almost choking on the word, "will I have dinner alone on a night like this?"

"Oh, William," she said quietly. When he looked up, he saw tears in her eyes. "Of course not. Don't you see, if I go now, your mother and father will spend more time with you. You and I, we're almost too close. It leaves other people out."

"The castle doesn't make any difference," said William, getting up. "I'm still going to figure out a way to make you stay."